Lady G. O.

The Ironmaster

Vol. III.

Lady G. O.

The Ironmaster
Vol. III.

ISBN/EAN: 9783337178314

Printed in Europe, USA, Canada, Australia, Japan

Cover: Foto ©Andreas Hilbeck / pixelio.de

More available books at **www.hansebooks.com**

THE BATTLES OF LIFE.

THE IRONMASTER.

VOL. III.

THE BATTLES OF LIFE.

THE IRONMASTER.

FROM THE FRENCH OF

GEORGES OHNET,

AUTHOR OF

"LA COMTESSE SARAH," "LISE FLEURON," ETC. ETC.

BY LADY G. O.

AUTHORIZED TRANSLATION.

IN THREE VOLUMES.
VOL. III.

LONDON:
WYMAN & SONS, 74–76, GREAT QUEEN ST.
LINCOLN'S-INN FIELDS.
1884.

WYMAN AND SONS, PRINTERS,
GREAT QUEEN STREET, LINCOLN'S-INN FIELDS,

THE IRONMASTER.

CHAPTER I.

THE Duke had not come of his own free will to instal himself at La Varenne. He could not bear the country. A Parisian in his soul, the plane-trees of the Boulevards and the chestnut-trees of the Champs-Elysées seemed to him quite sufficient verdure. His club, where he passed his afternoons and the greater part of his evenings, formed the basis of his life. He was in nowise contemplative and detested reading.

When his father-in-law escorted him with pride to the hot-houses of La Varenne, to show him a superb collection of orchids, that his gardener, a man to whom Moulinet spoke with deference, had reared at great expense, the Duke cast an absent glance upon the pots symmetrically arranged, murmured indifferently: "Very pretty." Then, with the tips of his fingers, detaching from its stem a marvellous flower, he placed it in his button-hole.

The gardener was appalled, at seeing plucked in such a disrespectful manner a flower of which the culture had cost so much money and labour. He let fall a pot of begonia that he was preparing to show, and, darting at Moulinet a severe look, went out in silence.

"Do you know that it is a flower worth fifteen louis that you have just gathered?"

smilingly said the late Judge at the Tribunal de Commerce.

"Indeed?" said the Duke with tranquillity. "Well, but I do not think it too dear for myself."

Moulinet looked askance at his son-in-law, but made no reply. In fact, he feared him. The Duke had a way of eyeing him from head to foot that over-awed him. Moulinet had said one evening to the foppish Maître Escandre: "Whatever we may do, we shall never be the equals of these people!" And although he had, above all since his electoral designs, equalizing tendencies, he did not feel himself on an even footing with the Duke.

Having so little succeeded with his hothouses, he hoped to make more impression with his stables. He had mustered there a dozen horses for riding and driving, of which his coachman spoke very highly, and, that he had paid for in proportion.

The outbuildings of La Varenne are imposing. They were built of brick, and in the Moorish style, which excessively pleased the late Judge at the Tribunal de Commerce. When he spoke of them, he said delightedly: "They much resemble the Alhambra and the new Collège Chaptal."

The court, upwards of two hundred yards square, is surrounded on its four sides by the buildings appropriated to the stables, to the coach-houses, to the saddle-room, and to the supply of forage. A massive door, framed by two stone pillars, ornamented by the heads of horses in bronze, gives access to the yard. Arcades run all the length of the buildings, form-ing a walk three yards in width, paved with flag-stones. Fences of wood, painted white, on which one can lean in order to see the horses exercised, separate each arcade.

The Duchess, in a gown of foulard, carrying, in a hand loaded with rings, a large red sunshade, her pretty brown head rising from a collar of *point de Venise*, accompanied her father and her husband to the stables. She crushed with her small shoe the braid of carefully-plaited straw bordering the litter, looked at each horse at liberty in his box, above which a metal plate was prepared for the name. The management of the stables obtained the approbation of the Duke, but the horses left him cold. The head coachman sought vainly for compliments. The Duke detected at a glance the defect of each animal, and gave cause for deep reflection to M. Moulinet.

In the evening there was a serious

explanation, from which the coachman discovered, that the son-in-law of M. Moulinet knew too much, for it to be possible in the future, to make his master pay six thousand francs for horses not worth more than eighteen hundred. The Duke summed up his opinion in a manner that ended by gaining for him the esteem of the stableman.

"Rob your master, my good fellow," said he; "that is quite natural; but do not get him laughed at!"

Having taken the Duke to visit his hot-houses and his stables, without more success for the one than for the other, the late Judge at the Tribunal de Commerce, found himself at the end of the distractions that he had kept in store for his son-in-law. The latter, between his wife and M. Moulinet, wearied himself wonderfully. Solitude became precious to

him. And every day, after breakfast, he
shut himself up in the smoking-room.
There, stretched upon the large divan of
Havanna leather, he slept idly. At the
end of a week of this existence, not being
able longer to support it, feeling imperti-
nences crowding, boiling, and rushing to
his lips, the Duke made known to his wife
and his father-in-law that pressing affairs
summoned him to Trouville, when Athénaïs
at once proposed to call at Pont-Avesnes.

This suggestion surprised the Duke,
and, at first sight, was disagreeable to
him. The recollection of Claire had been
gradually effaced from his heart, but that
of the Ironmaster remained there clear
and distinct. The woman had become
almost indifferent to him, but he cherished
rancour against the husband. For what?
He would have been at a loss to say.
Perhaps because he had been the accom-

plice in the affront that Claire had made the Duke publicly undergo. Perhaps because his disposition was quite opposed to that of de Bligny. Finally, he was instinctively hostile to him whom he continued to call "the blacksmith."

He was, however, curious to see how this marriage, concluded under such whimsical circumstances, had turned out. And he accompanied his father-in-law and his wife to the house of M. Derblay without requiring great entreaty. He said to himself: "My journey will only be delayed for a day, and I can show some attention to that poor Claire. I certainly owe her that."

He compassionated her, and pictured to himself a very singular idea of the life of her whom he ought to have married. He imagined it mean, narrow, and sordid, occupied exclusively with the cares of her household. A little more would have made him fancy his proud cousin, keeping the books of her husband, with sleeves of black glazed cotton half-way up her arms.

The Duke had only seen Pont-Avesnes in the darkness of night. On entering by daylight a handsome court, ornamented by a beautiful flower-garden in the French style, he was astonished at the aspect, majestic and severe, of the Château. The servants appeared to him well trained and not savouring at all of the Provinces. The salons struck him by their luxurious splendour. And he was forced to own to himself that the mode of life in the house of M. Derblay was most enviable. The apparition of Claire troubled him.

It was no longer herself. The woman that he had before his eyes was not only more beautiful than the Claire whom he had known. She was another: simple,

grave, with an authority in her glance
that embarrassed him. M. Derblay was
too well off not to displease considerably
the Duke. For the first time, he observed
that the Ironmaster was decorated.

Plunged into sudden reflection, Bligny
spoke but little, and with propriety; it
was owing to that reserve that the sus-
picions of Philippe were not immediately
aroused.

During the journey, from Pont-Avesnes
to La Varenne, the Duke was very taci-
turn. At dinner, he was too lively,
talking with feverish exuberance, bantering M. Moulinet, and exhibiting himself
as the best son-in-law in the world. His
apathy had abruptly left him. And he
spoke no more of the urgent affairs which
were calling him to Trouville.

But he shut himself up more than ever
in the smoking-room. Only, he no longer

slept. Extended upon the divan, he smoked, throughout the day, those cigarettes from the Levant which incite to reverie. He watched the blue smoke-wreaths slowly ascend to the ceiling, seeming to pursue, through their light and floating spirals, a fugitive shape. In a half obscurity, the face of Claire, such as he had just seen it, appeared to him. He closed his eyes and saw it perpetually.

Tormented by that vision, he wished to escape it by movement, and ordered to be saddled one of those horses for which M. Moulinet had paid so dear and that were worth so little money. And through the park he rode, allowing the reins to lie upon the neck of his horse.

It was four o'clock and the wood became full of vague sounds. The career of the vagabond rabbits made the leaves rustle in the underwood, and from time

to time a startled magpie flew to the top
of a great oak, raising its strident cry and
beating the air with its short wings. The
day had been burning. A delicious fresh-
ness came with the evening. Exquisite
odours arose from the earth and the
sun, sinking towards the west, pierced
with his rays of gold the foliage of the
trees.

Shaking off his torpor, the Duke spurred
his horse, which started at a gallop. Without being aware of it, he had left the park,
and now was riding in the middle of the
forest. The charming phantom, which
haunted his mind, always fled before him,
drawing him after it. His horse had
carried him to the verge of the plain. A
large, low wall, over which some heavy
branches were hanging, attracted his
attention. A wide vista, bordered by a
deep haha, was opened in the thick mass

of the trees. The Duke, mechanically, rode towards it. A carpet of turf was spread out before his eyes, and, quite at the other side, rose a vast white building. The Duke started. He recognised Pont-Avesnes.

Thus, chance led him towards her from whom he strove to fly. Would Fate re-unite those whom she had separated?

Bligny began to smile. He remembered what he had said to the Baron the night of the marriage: "Since Vulcan, black-smiths have had no chance!" He forgot that terrible hammer with which his interlocutor had menaced him. Besides, would fear prevent the Duke from seeking to gratify one of his caprices? He started his horse at a trot. And, his resolution being taken for the future, his mind relieved, he returned to La Varenne.

Nothing could be more threatening to

the repose of M. Derblay than the fresh
intentions of the Duke. Between the
cold gravity of Philippe and the cajoling
grace of Gaston, the young woman would
be in great difficulty, if not in serious
danger.

It was evident that the Ironmaster, by
showing to the Duke such quiet cordiality,
had a mental reservation. Nothing would
have been more easy for him than to
banish, by degrees, the kinsfolk of his
wife and to limit the intimate acquaint-
ance, which was from the first day
established, to the bare and ordinary
intercourse of mere neighbours. It was
not easy to take advantage of Philippe,
and that which he had decided was
executed exactly, and at all points. If,
then, he abandoned himself in this manner
to the encroaching intimacy of the Duke
and of the Duchess, it was, that it entered

into his projects to throw open to them
his house.

During the long hours that Philippe
had passed at the bed-side of the suffering
Claire, he criticised one by one the events
that preceded his marriage. He took
into consideration the animosity with
which Athénaïs had pursued her rival.
He gave to the Duchess her share of
responsibility. And the more guilty he
found her, the more he was inclined to
excuse Claire. Nevertheless, he deemed
it necessary not to depart from the rigour
with which he had till that time treated
his wife.

The combat that he had engaged in
with her must terminate in his victory.
But it was necessary to make the haughty
Claire undergo a decisive trial, and he
must take a terrible revenge for the
unmerited affront that she had inflicted

upon him. He had a presentiment that Athénaïs was destined to play her part in this dangerous game. The battle would be between the Duchess and Claire, between the Duke and himself. He foresaw it furious, full of perfidious ambushes, and of formidable surprises. It was not impossible that it would be decided by the death of a man.

Philippe had no hesitation. After all, what had he to lose? His life was compromised and his happiness lost. He could only gain by essaying the adventure. But, prudent as he was resolute, he wished to take his precautions and to do all to assure himself success. Finding Claire too isolated, inasmuch as, apparently, he could not undertake her defence, he thought of giving her a faithful ally, and invited the Baroness, to come with her husband, to pass a few weeks with them.

The forces would be thus equalized, and, the two parties once in presence of each other, there was only to await the attack.

From the first, it was easy to see that the Duchesse de Bligny had formed the design of revolutionizing this little peaceful corner of the Province. La Varenne became a mirthful centre, that re-echoed incessantly with the magnificence of the *fêtes*, through which Athénaïs was desirous of signalizing her arrival. Having been transplanted but lately to the country, she aspired to become its incontestable sovereign, by dint of pomp, of animation, and of eccentricity.

She had ordered from Paris two of her followers, the big La Brède and the little du Tremblaye, the most brilliant pair of trotters from her famous team of six. " La Brède and du Tremblaye," she laughingly said, " they would suffice for the country. One could harness them in turn, and with many bells, they would make a show! . . . "

In fact, La Brède and du Tremblaye,— those two inseparables who, dull enough taken singly, were wonderful when together, their two nullities becoming of value, in the same way that two negatives make an affirmative,—had arrived with fresh ideas for a cotillon, and the materials for lawn-tennis and polo in their luggage. And, as if the demon of Paris had emerged from their valises, hardly had they set foot in La Varenne, when life there became furious.

Besançon found an orchestra of ten musicians to furnish to the Duchess, for they danced every Saturday at the Château. The Jurassienne young people heard with astonishment that Madame de Bligny had the intention of entertaining the whole country. From all the surrounding châteaux, Berlins, britzskas, wagonets, every whimsical construction from the hands of a carriage-maker, of which a few specimens dated from the Restoration, scattered themselves, rattling and jingling, over the road to La Varenne. The country proprietors high-coloured, with muscles hard as the rocks of their mountains, set themselves to handle the racket at lawn-tennis; to drive, at a gallop over the green-sward, the ball at polo,— while giving each other hard blows with the sticks upon the head,—and to waltz for whole evenings with untiring vigour.

" Acknowledge then, Duchess, they are tough fellows, your Provincials," cried the big La Brède: "they carry off their partners like feathers, and they never

rest! I have almost a fancy to import
a few of them for my winter season in
Paris . . . They would do well to lead
our cotillons . . . And I believe that
they would be at a premium upon the
Place . . . ''

"Yes, but here is the misfortune," said
the little du Tremblaye. "The muscular
and rubicund provincial generally succeeds
badly with us. At the end of six months
he loses his colour and becomes more
enervated than the Parisian himself . . .
A bad species for acclimation! . . . ''

Whilst the two Parisians devoted themselves to these profound considerations
upon the raising and transplanting of provincial dancers, the ten musicians were
playing impetuously in the salons of La
Varenne. The young people from Besançon and its environs, careless of appreciation, and contemptuous of criticism,

danced, with a satisfaction that rejoiced the heart of Moulinet.

The late Judge at the Tribunal de Commerce, had expanded on seeing his daughter move with that impassioned ardour the best society of his district. The candidate said to himself: "So many guests, so many electors." He urged the Duchess forward in that path by opening for her an unlimited credit. And while the girls and the women danced, he undertook the fathers and the husbands. Moulinet had, however, one care: neither the Préfet, nor the General commanding the fortress of Besançon, came to the *soirées* at La Varenne. Perhaps the centre appeared too aristocratic to the representative of the Civil administration. As to the head of the Military administration, he had just been reprimanded for having suffered the garrison to carry arms at the Procession, and thought it prudent to abstain from showing his decorations in the salons of the Duchess.

"What harm can it do to thee if the Préfet does not come," asked Athénaïs of Moulinet, who was very troubled, "if all his subordinates are for thee? Have him satirized in the *Courrier!* Let them relate a ludicrous anecdote about him! Stay, wilt thou that I make La Brède write the article? It shall be witty. As to the General, he is a cipher: his soldiers do not vote!"

Athénaïs had a much graver subject for discontent than her father. Madame Derblay excused herself from coming to the Saturday *soirées.* She said that she was still too suffering to keep late hours. The Duchess, whose sole end, in giving her *fêtes,* had been to constrain Claire to assist at them, devoured with difficulty her rage.

She had impulses of temper which troubled the gaiety of her surroundings. Not to crush her rival with all her luxury, not to plunge a thousand daggers into her heart, by exhibiting herself to Claire leaning on the arm of him whom she had hoped to marry, not to see her start every time that they called Athénaïs Madame la Duchesse, it was to lose all the pleasure that she had promised herself. The hatred of the young woman, which would perhaps have been calmed by the spectacle of the humiliation of Claire, by the revelation of her tortures, was, on the contrary, intensified by the resistance that the latter knew how to offer, by the haughty tranquillity that dwelt upon her forehead.

Claire went to dine once at La Varenne and comported herself very skilfully. The petulant and encroaching Duchess, near that noble and elegant woman, appeared that which she in reality was: a little person, rather under-bred, doing and saying all that entered her brain, with the audacity of the parvenue millionaire. One could see at a glance the difference, and the advantage was for Claire.

Athénaïs felt it, and promised herself terrible reprisals. That dark young woman, with a charming face, a quick eye and a pleasant smile, was one of the most malevolent upon the earth! She would have been capable, had there been no grave liability to incur, of dashing vitriol in the face of that adorable Claire, so as to disfigure her once for all, and to burn without possible remedy the beautiful eyes, pure and tranquil, in which she read so much disdain.

That which above all irritated the Duchess, was the good understanding that seemed to exist between M. and Madame

Derblay. The husband was courteous, tender, and attentive; the wife full of deference and of affection. One could not be deceived in the smile of Claire, when Philippe was near her, and protecting her with all his power; she loved him. And certainly she was loved. How could the Ironmaster fail to adore a creature so perfect, uniting, in an exquisite harmony, physical grace and moral beauty? Moreover, had he not married her for love? Passing over all the humiliating circumstances of the situation, accepting a penniless woman, and one who was forsaken by the Duke. And he was simply happy in possessing her, as if indeed she had been a rare treasure!

Thus, it was the destiny of Claire to be always loved. While Fate had decided that Athénaïs should find men indifferent to her. Without doubt they courted her.

But what were these adulations, these
gallantries of the salon, these fleeting
fancies that she inspired, compared to the
love sincere, deep, unalterable, that Claire
had the gift of winning ?

In the transport of her jealousy,
Athénaïs occupied herself especially with
M. Derblay. She tried seriously to please
him, and monopolized him during part of
the evening. The Duchess really admired
him very much. With his complexion
bronzed by the fresh air, his black hair
cut short over the forehead, and his large
brown eyes, he resembled an Arab.
Athénaïs felt herself suddenly disquieted.
Never had any man caused in her a similar
emotion. She thought that, if ever she
were capable of being captivated by any
one, it would be by Philippe. And
rejoicing, at the idea of the affliction that
it would cause to Claire, she yielded to

her natural coquetry with an animation that surprised herself.

She soon experienced a diabolical joy at seeing Claire gloomy, troubled, following with anguish the adroit and skilful wiles to which Athénaïs was abandoning herself. The Duchess read her pain upon the face of the woman whom she hated, and, from that time, comprehended that she had discovered the weak point in the armour, through which it would be possible for her to strike a mortal blow.

It is true, the attitude of Philippe was that of a well-bred man, who sees himself the object of the flattering attentions of his hostess. He received with perfect equanimity the very accentuated advances of the Duchess, allowed her to take his arm in order to survey the salons, and conversed with ease. He was just sufficiently in earnest to appear very agreeable, and just sufficiently cold that it could not be said he was, with the Duchess, otherwise than with all other women.

Yet, master of himself as he was, an attentive observer would have discovered that he was a prey to violent agitation. During the time that the Duchess, flaunting like a young pea-fowl, had seized upon him, and was showing him the salon, the conservatories, he saw Bligny quietly approach Claire, bend over the back of her chair, and smilingly talk with her. It was the first time that he had seen Gaston and Claire near each other, exchanging their thoughts without a witness. He shuddered, and a burning flush mounted to his temples. For a moment, he suffered so cruelly that his arm contracted, pressing violently the hand of the Duchess. She regarded him with astonishment. They were in a small conservatory that Moulinet called " the tropics," in which were unfolding themselves, gorgeous in the midst of a damp heat, the poisonous plants of India and of Africa.

" What ails you?" asked the Duchess, giving back to the arm of her cavalier a slight pressure.

And she began to smile.

" The powerful odour of these plants and the heat of the conservatory made me giddy," answered the Ironmaster, regaining his calmness. " Let us return to the salon, if you are willing?"

And, slowly conducting the Duchess, he returned, keeping under his eyes the Duke and Claire, who were still conversing.

After dinner, the Duke did not appear. He led away his guests to the smoking-room, and put before them the most varied

collection of cigars and cigarettes. At
the end of half-an-hour, he made a pretext
of his duties, as master of the house, and
left the smokers in the midst of a thick
cloud. He wished to become reconciled
with Claire. But being acquainted with
the impetuous temper of the young
woman, he feared to risk accosting her
openly. Besides, he felt himself constrained in her presence, and, daring as
he was, hesitated to speak, feeling sure,
that the first words he addressed to her
would be of vital importance to their
future relations.

Perhaps it would be better to refrain as
yet, and, to leave time to harden the
ground before venturing on it. But
Bligny had reached to that point of
cynical egotism that he was not able to
delay the gratification of one of his
caprices. He advanced then, speaking to

his friends, making short pauses near the ladies, contracting, like a bird of prey, the circles that he was describing around Claire. He arrived in this way behind her, took a step, and bending towards the young woman, whose warm perfume he inhaled :

" Do you feel quite well this evening ? " said he in a caressing voice. " I come almost tremblingly to ask of you tidings, for I fear to be so unhappy that you do not see me approach you without displeasure."

Claire turned quickly, regarding the Duke straight in the face :

" And why should I see you with displeasure ? " replied she fearlessly. " Should I have come to your house, if I had with regard to you the sentiments that you attribute to me ? "

The Duke shook his head with melancholy :

"This is the first time that we have the opportunity of speaking freely, since your marriage," continued he, "and I see that we are not yet going to speak the truth. It will be one of the griefs of my life, having conducted myself badly to you, not to be able to explain to you the reasons which may perhaps justify me."

"But you do not require to justify yourself, believe me," said Claire with tranquillity . . . "Have I reproached you ? And do you really think that you deserve reproach ? Let me tell you that it would be a proof of wonderful fatuity."

"You lighten my conscience of a very heavy weight," replied the Duke. "My marriage was one of the fatal necessities of Parisian life. On an unlucky day I found myself in such a situation that it was necessary to choose between my happiness and my honour. I had two obligations to discharge. But, while satisfying one, I was compelled to forfeit the other. I sacrificed my love, to save my name. That is, Claire, what I was determined to tell you . . ."

"In other words, M. Moulinet plucked you from a very thorny affair, and, from gratitude, you married his daughter . . . With several millions of dowry ! . . . Nonsense, Duke, " *La Pénitence est douce*," as the song says . . . And more, if I have well understood it, you have, in order to support you under that trial, the feeling of having accomplished a duty . . . You must then be happy . . . And you see me charmed at it . . ."

Under the goad of these ironical words, the Duke started :

" And you," said he brusquely, " are you happy ? "

" You are the only person who has not the right to ask it of me ! " exclaimed Claire proudly.

At the same moment, the Duchess returned with Philippe. The Duke, with a movement of the head, showed to his cousin, Athénaïs leaning on the arm of the Ironmaster. And, seeing Claire disturbed and pale, he cast at her a profoundly mocking glance :

" You deserve to be better loved," said he.

And, bowing, he slowly walked away.

Claire shivered at the thought that the Duke had been able to divine her secret. Thus, he called in question the happiness that she wished to establish, in the eyes of the world, at the price of so much dissimulation. She foresaw what dangers she

would have to encounter, should the Duke
have the evil inspiration of occupying himself with her. How could she continue
the work of conquering the affections of
her husband? How could she prevent
her husband from being troubled by the
proceedings of the Duke? And herself,
engaged in a battle with this dangerous
assailant, how could she be at liberty to
fight the Duchess, whose audacious
coquetry she already saw entangling
Philippe?

She resolved to fly. And making a
sign to her husband which brought him
quickly to her, Claire begged him to ask
for the carriage. Then, cutting short the
caressing protestations of Athénaïs, and
addressing a cold salutation to the Duke,
the young woman hurried Philippe away,
with as much precipitation, as if the
Château had been in flames.

When they were in their coupé, rolling over the resounding road, on a clear and mild night, Claire believed herself saved. She did not fear to interrogate Philippe, and, turning towards him :

"How did you find the Duchess?"

"Charming" . . . replied Philippe absently.

Claire sank into her corner with a gesture of vexation that the obscurity hid from Philippe. One single word had struck her : "Charming." She did not notice the accent of profound indifference with which it had been said.

"We will return no more to La Varenne," said Claire to herself. "I should suffer too much."

At the same moment, Philippe, plunged in a deep reverie, saw pass before his eyes the vision of the graceful figure of the

Duke, bending before Claire, and, with a perfidious smile, murmuring tender words in her ear. And his throat dry, his eyes threatening, the Ironmaster clenched his hand.

They did not again go to La Varenne. Fifteen days later, they returned to M. Moulinet, to the Duke and to the Duchess, the dinner that they had received, and opposed persistent refusals to the increasing politeness of their neighbours.

Athénaïs, exasperated, found La Brède without spirit and du Tremblaye without imagination. She waltzed without pleasure with the young men of the neighbourhood. Moulinet, pronounced fruitlessly at the Flower Show of La Varenne, to which he had succeeded in having himself named President, a discourse, which plunged into profound drowsiness those of the hearers that it did not reduce to subdued merriment.

There were fire-works, tournaments upon the Avesnes, they crowned *Rosières*, with the accompaniment of music by the *Lyre* of Besançon. They led the life, gay, noisy, fatiguing, that Athénaïs adored. But nothing could satisfy her. Madame Derblay was not there to witness her triumphs.

The Marquise, established upon the heights of Beaulieu, like a solitary and mournful turtle-dove, had not set foot in the house of her niece by marriage. The absence of M. and of Madame Derblay began to be remarked. Comments were made. And the Baronne de Préfont, that talkative person, having arrived at the house of Claire, Athénaïs foresaw the moment when the world would recognise a quarrel between La Varenne and Pont-Avesnes. It was necessary at all risks to break the ice that had grown thick, in menacing fields, between the two young households. A pastime almost public, to which the principal people of the country could be invited, would alone be able to serve as a pretext.

It was La Brède, who, accidentally and with the sole intention of diverting himself, like all inspired men, furnished to the Duchess the occasion so eagerly sought. He proposed a Paper-Chase, in the woods of La Varenne and of Pont-Avesnes. They could call together the authorities, civil and military. The officers of the garrison would receive invitations, and all the world would follow the chase either on horseback or in carriages. A colossal luncheon must be prepared at the *Rond-point* of the Ponds. In a word, they would give a sportive *fête*, that should be talked of in society and named in the journals of Paris.

Athénaïs was within a little of embracing La Brède for this godsend of genius, and despatching her father in advance with invitations, setting the entire household to cut small pieces of paper, the Duchess herself went to Pont-Avesnes, and returned radiant, with a favourable answer.

CHAPTER II.

THE Rond-point of the Ponds is situated on the outskirts of the woods of Pont-Avesnes and of those of La Varenne. A number of stagnant pools,—covered by reeds and by plants with large leaves, stretching their glossy stalks to the surface of the water, like sleeping serpents,— prolonged for four or five hundred yards, has given its name to the Rond-point. The lower branches of the oaks droop over as if trying to reach the cool water. And the leaves falling every year in the autumn, have formed, by decaying all along the margin, a thick mire to which the wild boars resort, in the early morning, to wallow deliciously. Palings painted white, barring,

on ordinary occasions, the roads to the
forest, enclose an open space upwards
of two hundred yards in extent, carpeted
by grass thick and soft as velvet.

Enormous beech - trees, with greyish
trunks, and thick foliage, encircle this
Rond-point, spreading over it a dense
shadow. The eight roads, twenty yards
in width, terminating at the open space,
straight and bordered by red tinted heather,
lose themselves in the depths of the forest.
It is a place full of silence and of mystery.
The sun flashes his rays on the waters
rippled by the breeze and the sky mirrors
in them its tranquil azure. For shooting
in the forest, the place is excellent. The
roe-buck, wearied by the ardent pursuit
of the hounds, comes to refresh in the
pools his trembling legs, and to imbibe
there, while drinking, a fresh vigour. A
sportsman posted upon the steep bank of

a pool, behind one of the great oaks, can
find there the longed-for opportunity to
cry: " *Hallali !* "

M. Moulinet, a passionate lover of
Nature, seduced by the beauty of the
landscape, has dishonoured the prospect
by constructing there a Chinese Kiosque.

In the centre of this vast clearing, a
table laid in the open air, served by footmen in dress liveries, offered to the guests
of the Duchess the necessary refreshment
before undertaking a long ride. For an
hour, La Brède, coupled with his faithful
du Tremblaye, had been hurrying through
the underwood, scattering slips of paper
which were to indicate the trail, taking
it on in front, returning upon his track,
multiplying the back scent, preparing
checks with fatiguing conscientiousness.

By all the roads leading to the Rond-
point, were arriving horsemen, horse-

women, breaks and calashes. The light
toilettes of the women sheltering themselves under their many - coloured sun-
shades, the blue *dolmans* and red trowsers
of the Hussars, formed bright spots against
the sombre verdure of the trees. The
horses, held by keepers dressed in green
cloth, and wearing round caps, stretched
towards the ground, covered by lush grass,
their greedy mouths; stirrups rang against
each other, there were bursts of shrill
neighing, champagne corks flew gaily,
allowing the wine to run foaming into the
glasses.

Compressed in her short-skirted black
habit, flicking, in her gloved hand, a riding-
whip the handle of which was ornamented
by an enormous cat's-eye, Athénaïs, with
a gaiety, an ease and a surprising grace,
was doing the honours of the forest to the
arrivals.

Upon the cushions, of the great mail-coach of the Duke, thrown upon the grassy slope, the ladies were seated. Moulinet, wearing a blue coat and pearl grey gloves, at ten o'clock in the morning, was monopolizing the Baron, for whom he evinced an oppressive affection. The Duke exhibited himself in an English hunting costume, scarlet coat, white buckskin breeches, cap of black velvet ornamented at the back by a green knot : his colours, his blazon on a field sinople. Philippe, in a black coat as usual, had merely added breeches of grey velvet, with gaiters to correspond.

Claire and the Baroness, as if in uniform, each wore a habit of blue cloth, with a small round hat adorned by a black plume. They were adorable thus. Madame de Préfont, elegant and slender, Claire, tall and superb, her beautiful shoulders and bosom moulded in the simple and unornamented *corsage* of her habit.

Suzanne, waited on by Octave, was dipping a biscuit in a glass of Malaga, not losing sight of her pony, of which her brother, with paternal attention, had tightened the girth and examined the curb, whilst Bachelin, unharnessing tranquilly his horse for riding and driving, aided a keeper to put on the saddle that he had brought under the seat of his cabriolet. The sun gilded the woods, casting a glowing light over this brilliant picture. The air was light and fresh. It was pleasant to live.

"Monsieur Derblay! . . ." cried Athénaïs suddenly, forsaking the so-much-desired Préfet with whom she was conversing.

And as Philippe came to her, composedly, without precipitation:

"Do you not think that it is time to set out? It is at least an hour since those gentlemen started with their papers, and they went at a good pace, we must gallop fast to overtake them."

"*Mon Dieu*, Madame," answered Philippe, "I must own to you that I am but little acquainted with this kind of performance. I should fear to give advice. Apply rather to Pontac who, in his office of *Louvetier*, ought to be well versed in the subject . . ."

And, with a sign, Philippe pointed out a tall young man in a huntsman's costume laced with silver, wearing a three-cornered hat, having a hunting-knife at his side, and a horn *à la Dampierre* over his shoulder. As if he had only awaited an opportunity to introduce himself, the

Viçomte de Pontac advanced to the centre of the Rond-point, and, bowing before Madame de Bligny with English stiffness :

"Duchess, I am at your orders," said he. "And if you will commit to me the management of the hunt, I shall do my best to put, before two o'clock, Messieurs La Brède and du Tremblaye to their last resources. Is it your pleasure that we sound the start? My *piqueur* is there . . . Ho! Ho! Bistocq!"

A great fellow, arrayed in a braided jacket, gaitered with tawny leather, a rubicund nose shining in the midst of his sun-tanned face like a strawberry upon the earth, emerged from a group of servants, walking with difficulty and leading after him a tall raw-boned horse, badly groomed, whose bridle was passed over his arm. Arrived at six paces from M. de Pontac, he stopped, and, taking the position of a soldier without arms, raised his hand to the peak of his cap, and waited that they might ask of him his report.

"Do you desire that I interrogate him?" asked the Vicomte of the Duchess.

"Certainly," replied Athénaïs, enchanted by the solemnity of the proceeding.

"*Ma chère*, look at her!" murmured the Baroness in an audible voice, "she gives herself the airs of a queen! And Pontac, who plays his part in earnest! All this to run after little pieces of paper! How amusing it is!"

"The start will be at the Heronry," said Bistocq; "it is there that the scent begins. There is a heap of paper as large as my hand. No occasion to break a branch! Those gentlemen were without doubt afraid that we should not find them easily enough! . . . They might as well have put a journal . . . The animals . . . excuse me . . . those gentlemen escaped through the trees, they jumped the Pavé-Neuf, took to the plain at the Vente-au-Sergent, re-entered the forest at Belle-Empleuse, went ahead at the foot of the hill of La Haie, took to their back scent at La Boulottière . . ."

"Halt!" said M. de Pontac laughing, "if we let thee go on, thou will give us the whole itinerary of the chase . . ."

"There would be a chance of it!" said the *piqueur*, winking. "You must not think that a foolish person can imitate like that the deer . . . It is only through using the brains that that would be easy!" murmured he with a bantering air. "And besides, in order to succeed better, you have set to work two!"

The Duchess began to laugh, and turning to Pontac:

"He is droll, your *piqueur*," said she. "Papa, give a louis to this good fellow . . . Thanks to him, La Brède and du Tremblaye will find it necessary to improve their talent, if not they will be taken quickly . . ."

"*Hallali courant!*" said Pontac . . . "Duchess, shall we sound the departure?"

"Sound, Vicomte."

Pontac, turning his horn with the left hand, placed himself in the centre of the open space, and inflating his cheeks as if he wished to uproot the trees of the forest, he cast to the echoes the ringing notes of the *fanfare*.

"My compliments, Vicomte," said the Duchess. "You have a wonderful talent . . ."

"It is hereditary in my family," answered Pontac, with thoughtful gravity. "For three centuries, from father to son, we have sounded the horn!"

And shaking his head with the airs of a superior man, the Vicomte walked towards his horse.

In a moment the whole company was in motion, those who were riding, with foot in stirrup, those who followed in carriages, upon the cushions of their vehicles of all kinds. A universal impulse hurried away the mass of the guests towards the wide drives extending to the Heronry. The dull thud of the feet of horses galloping over the mossy road, was already rapidly becoming lost in the distance, while Bistocq, guiding the pursuit at the full trot of his raw-boned mount, sounded the triumphant call of the tracker.

"Monsieur Derblay, you who are so well

acquainted with the country," said the Duchess with a smile, "will you be so amiable as to show me the way? We will let the main body of the hunt precede us. You have a good horse, I also; we will make a short cut through the woods, and take them in advance . . ."

"But, Duchess, is there not Pontac, who knows better how to lead you than myself?" said Philippe.

"No," exclaimed the Duchess merrily, "it is you that shall give me a lead, at least, unless you refuse me? But I do not believe you capable of it . . ."

The Ironmaster bowed without reply. Claire, standing at a short distance, had heard, while trembling with anger, the audacious solicitation of Athénaïs. Tears of mortification came to her eyes, and, without being conscious of it, she convulsively pressed the arm of the astonished Baroness.

"Thou art going with us, is it not so?" asked the Duchess, turning to Claire.

The young woman inclined gently her beautiful saddened face, and with a calm voice :

"No! I have presumed too much on my strength in thinking that I could follow the chase on horseback . . . I shall go in the carriage . . ."

And Claire, darting a pitiful look at her husband, appeared to supplicate him not to abandon her.

"Does it vex thee that I take away thy husband?" asked the Duchess with feigned solicitude. Then, laughingly : "Art thou a little jealous?"

"No!" answered Claire, not wishing to acknowledge, so publicly, her powerlessness and her grief.

" Then, to horse ! " said Athénaïs joyously, hastening to complete her victory.

Claire, her heart wrung, watched the departure of her husband; she had for a moment the idea of calling him, of detaining him, and said :

" Philippe ! "

The Ironmaster turned quickly, and coming to her :

" What is it ? " said he. " Are you suffering ? Do you desire anything ? "

Without doubt, if the young woman had appealed to him, her husband would have remained with her. Perhaps many torments would have been thus avoided. Pride, still more powerful than love, arrested the supplicating words upon the lips of Claire. She shook her head, and, with a harsh manner, her mouth contracted, making a gesture of disdain :

"No," answered she, "I ail nothing, I wish for nothing! Go!"

Philippe went. At that moment, Claire united him in the growing hatred that she was accumulating against Athénaïs. She was seized by one of those furies during which one slays.

Placing her foot upon the sloping bank of the ditch, the Duchess raised her skirt. Her leg, compressed in a boot of grey buckskin, appeared slender and elegant. With a sign she showed to M. Derblay the strap of her spur which had become loose. The Ironmaster stooped, and, without speaking, fixed upon the arched instep the narrow thong of leather ornamented by links of steel, and re-fastened the buckle set near the heel. Alluring and confident, the Duchess supporting herself against him, touched his shoulder with the pommel of her riding whip, as if to thoroughly establish her power.

"Ah! But what does that mean?" murmured the Baroness.

And, fixing her eyes upon her friend, she saw her so pale, so trembling, that she feared to continue her interrogation.

Raised by the strong arm of Philippe, the Duchess sprang into her saddle. She gathered up her reins, made with her hand a haughty gesture to her crushed rival, and starting her horse at a gallop, cleared with a bound the ditch separating the open space from the tall trees. Philippe followed, and, at the end of an instant, their indistinct shadows were lost in the depths of the forest.

"Will you allow me to stay with you?" gently murmured a voice near Claire, standing motionless, depressed, watching the flight of the two riders, as if they were carrying away her happiness. She turned. The Duke was at her side. The young woman suppressed a cry of anger, and tearing off her gloves, her forehead frowning, her eyes lowered :

" Leave me," said she, " I wish to be alone." And taking the arm of the Baroness, she walked towards the Pools while the Duke rode after his guests, guided by the horn which was sounding in the distance.

Octave and Suzanne, walking with slow steps, careless of the chase, followed the green margin of the water. Their horses, fastened to the same tree, playfully caressed each the neck of the other, or drew with difficulty into their mouths, encumbered by the steel bits, the young shoots of the branches. The Baron, left to his own devices, seated himself apart, and, with the aid of a small hammer, broke little chips from specimens of mineral that he had picked up by the road-side.

The two young women, without speaking, arrived at the Kiosque. It was surrounded by benches and they seated themselves. A deep silence, succeeding the movement and the noise, spread over the woods. A faint breeze was stirring the reeds, in the midst of which dragon-flies darted glittering in their uncertain flight. The Baroness bent her eyes upon her friend. Claire had regained her self-possession. A slight trembling of the lips alone indicated, the still persistent agitation of her nerves. Fearing to have been read, even by the Baroness, she lowered her head and turned away her face, moving with an indifferent air the sand with her foot.

"Well! What does all this mean?" cried the Baroness, incapable of longer restraining herself, "I come to thy house

thinking to find people steeped in pastoral
_tranquillity, and I fall amongst alterca-
tions, skirmishings. Thy husband gallops
off with Athénaïs, the Duke comes humbly
to offer to thee his society . . . "

"It is as in a quadrille," said Claire,
laughing nervously, "one changes partners . . ."

The Baroness became grave and, taking
the hand of her cousin :

"Why dost thou try to deceive me?
Dost thou believe me so giddy that I cannot comprehend all that is passing within
thee? Claire, thou art not happy!"

"I! and how can I not be? I live in
the midst of luxury, of sound, of animation. I have relations who adore me,
friends who surround me, a husband who
leaves me my liberty . . . Thou knowest
that it is of that I had dreamed. How
can I not be happy?"

" Well! my poor dear, what thou didst formerly dream, causes thy despair to-day. Thy husband leaves thee thy liberty, but he has resumed his own. And when thou seest him with another, thy heart is torn . . . From pride thou wouldst deny it, but thy grief betrays thee. No, thou art not happy! Thou canst not be, for thou ar jealous!"

" I!" exclaimed Claire with anger.

She burst into a fit of painful laughter, that ended by a sob. Her eyes filled with tears, and, sinking into the arms of her friend, her face crimsoning with shame, she wept bitterly.

The Baroness allowed her to ease her over-full heart of its sadness. Then, seeing her more calm, drew from her the sorrowful secret of her rupture with Philippe.

Madame de Préfont was dismayed. She understood the torments that Claire was

enduring, and had a suspicion of those
suffered by the Ironmaster. She divined
the horror of the contrast between the
public existence of these two beings and
their home life.   Outwardly, splendour,
the appearance of gaiety and of tenderness.
Inwardly, silence, coldness and solitude.
In society these two unfortunates played a
part. And they played it well. From that
time the Baroness had but one thought:
to work for the reconciliation of these
two, separated through a deplorable folly.
And she wished to penetrate into the heart
of Claire.

"But when thy husband nursed thee
with such devotion," said she, "didst
thou not for an instant have the thought
of speaking to him, and of trying to reunite
the broken bonds?"

"Yes," answered Claire reddening.
"I did not know what was passing within

me. I no longer felt myself the same person. Was it gratitude for his care, or a juster appreciation of his character that attracted me to him? But, when he was not there, involuntarily I sought him. When he was near me, I did not look at him, and yet I saw him. He was so severe, so grave, that I did not dare to speak to him . . . Oh! if he had encouraged me!"

"He has never done so?"

"No! He is as proud as myself, and more resolute . . . No, there is nothing to hope, we are separated for ever!"

"Moreover, he has taken willingly to his part, so far as I see. And our fine little Duchess Moulinet . . ."

"Do not blame Philippe!" quickly interrupted Claire . . . "It is she who throws herself impudently at his head . . . She pursues me incessantly . . . After my betrothed, my husband! What a triumph! Is it not? And how to tear him from her? What to do to defend myself? Have not I, only, the right to him? Is he not mine?"

"*Dame,* frankly, he is rather more thine than hers!"

"Oh! But let her beware!" said Claire with anger. "I have already suffered too much, through her. The most enduring patience has its limits. And if she forces me beyond them, I do not know what I shall do, but it will be something desperate which shall destroy one or the other of us!"

"There! *Ma belle,* calm thyself. I am here now in thy game, and I answer to thee that we shall conquer this delicious Athénaïs . . . She is a monopolist, dost thou see? In that she resembles her family. Her father formerly swept off the stakes on sugars. Her speciality is husbands. She must have them all. *Mon Dieu!* How I wish that she would take it into her head to captivate the Baron! How I should amuse myself! "

And, with a sign, the young woman showed to her friend the dear Préfont, always planted in the same spot, whiling away the long pause by gathering together little pebbles, with which he was cramming his pockets. Claire could not prevent herself from smiling. The image of Philippe passed before her eyes. He was not, a docile and patient servant, but a master imperious and formidable.

"The situation, we cannot disguise it, is grave," continued the Baroness. "If one could have an explanation, an arrangement would be easy. But, by speaking, one exposes oneself to a repulse, which one would resent, and then; all is ended!

. . . We must, therefore, make use of
diplomacy . . . Nothing will take from
me the idea that thy husband adores
thee, but will not let thee see it. A man
such as he loves only once, and it is for his
whole life. Hast thou carefully regarded
M. Derblay? He is stubborn. His firmness amounts to obstinacy . . . With that
character, thou wilt only be able to disarm
him by humiliating thyself."

"Ah! I should not hesitate to do
it . . . Nothing would be to me too
great a sacrifice in order to gain him. But
if he were to see, in my advances, a new
caprice?"

"Therefore we must wait, for a favourable opportunity, to play that important
game. If it does not present itself, we
will make it. But, for Heaven's sake, do
not keep that gloomy and despairing
mien. Thou wilt cause too much joy to

our dear friend. Remember that to all
the world thou art happy, and give to
thyself the appearance of happiness until
thou art so in reality."

Claire sighed. She, the untamable,.
who formerly prided herself on sur--
mounting every obstacle, now doubted
her power and had no confidence in her
will.

"It seems to me that, for the last half
hour, we have been talking in a very
serious fashion," said the Baroness; this
conjugal psychology has made my head
quite heavy. If thou wilt take my advice,.
we should gallop a little. And then, I
wish to see what the fine little Duchess.
Moulinet is doing with thy husband . . .
Wilt thou come?"

"No," answered Claire sadly, "I am
tired, I shall stay here. My brother and
Suzanne do not seem more disposed than

myself to follow the chase . . . They will bear me company . . ."

Octave and the young girl were returning slowly. They were no longer conversing. The Marquis, rather more serious than was customary with him. Suzanne, her head bent, and smiling at her happy thoughts. They arrived in this manner at the place where they had left their horses. The young man unfastened the bridles, and turning to Suzanne:

" You permit me to tell my sister ? "

Suzanne bowed her head in sign of assent, saying :

" Tell her, I wish it. You know how much she loves us. She will be delighted."

" Very well! You will go with the Baron and Baroness. I will stay with Claire and confide to her our secret."

And holding to' Suzanne his hands crossed, in which she placed her small foot, he put her quickly in the saddle. The young girl raised her eyes, regarded Octave, a little longer perhaps than was necessary, exchanged with him a pressure of the hand through which she expressed to him all that she feared to say. And touching with her whip the shoulder of her pony, with a bound she was in the centre of the Rond-point.

The horn, sounded in the forest, was drawing near, giving wings to La Brède and to du Tremblaye.

" Now, Baron, to horse ! " said Madame de Préfont to her husband.

" I am at your orders, *ma chère amie*," answered the amiable man tearing himself from the contemplation of his minerals . . . " It is very curious : fancy, that I shall not be astonished if the rocks of this bed

contain alum. I must speak of it to
M. Derblay. One could perhaps com-
pete with the alum-pits of Italy . . . You
know them ? . . . Near Civita-Vecchia . . .
I took you to visit them during our honey-
moon . . . It would be a fine thing. So
much sulphate of alumina is necessary in
the fabrication of paper . . ."

"Yes, Baron, yes," said the young
woman, with a sudden tenderness, "you
are an angel ! And what is more a learned
angel ! Stay, kiss my hand !"

"With pleasure," said the Baron,
without losing any of his usual tranquillity.

And he carried to his lips the carefully
gloved hand of his wife. The Baroness
cast a circular glance around her, made
her horse prance tumultuously, saluted
with her hand Claire and Octave; then,
turning to Suzanne :

" Are you coming with us, Suzanne ? . . . Yes ? . . . Then, *en route !* . . ."

And followed by her husband and the young girl, she set off at a great rate.

Octave and Claire, motionless, watched them disappear in the distance. There was a short silence. The young man, thoughtful and a little oppressed by emotion and by the confidence he was about to make. The young woman, meditating on her late conversation with the Baroness, and weighing with a vague anguish her chances of success in this difficult enterprise. The voice of the Marquis drew her from her contemplation.

" Claire," said he, " I have great news to tell thee."

And as his sister made a gesture of surprise, interrogating him with a glance :

" Suzanne and I, we love each other,"
added he in a lower tone.

The melancholy face of Claire was
illumined like a stormy sky suddenly
traversed by a ray of sunshine. She
stretched out her hands to her brother,
drawing him quickly to a seat near, her
nerves deliciously troubled, her mind
sympathetic, eager to know all, and
already seeing dawn that favourable
opportunity which ought to facilitate a
reconciliation with Philippe. There, in
the silence, with ecstasy, Octave related to
her the simple, yet already long romance,
of these two hearts, which by degrees had
taken possession of each other. Sincere
and placid loves, full of pure tenderness,
and born gently, without effort, without
agitation, like beautiful flowers, under the
blue sky.

" Thou hast so much influence over

Philippe," said the Marquis to his sister : "speak to him for me, make him give Suzanne to me. He has long been acquainted with my ideas. He knows that I count as nothing the advantages of birth, and that I rely upon making a position for myself. In fine, be eloquent, try to convince him, for thou hast my happiness in thy hands."

Claire became suddenly grave. That influence attributed to her by Octave, she did not possess. Never, since that fatal night, the starting-point of so many griefs, had she exchanged a single serious word with Philippe. At Pont-Avesnes they only saw each other at the hour of meals. Before the servants, they spoke little and always of common things. And without any preamble, without preparation, without encouragement, it would be necessary to broach so important a subject ! She did

not hesitate however: her happy confidence had returned to her. She had a
presentiment of victory.

Already disquieted by the silence of
Claire, the Marquis, like all lovers prompt
to see difficulties, cried:

"Thou wilt not at least refuse to charge
thyself with my cause?"

"No, certainly," replied the young
woman with a brave smile, "be tranquil,
I will plead for thee as for myself."

"Oh! Let me thank thee!" said
Octave. And, throwing his arm round
the shoulders of his sister, he embraced
her tenderly.

"These are my fees!" said Claire with
a gaiety that for the last year had not been
remarked in her. "One can see that thou
hast confidence: thou payest in advance.
But, go thou to find her, now that thou
hast owned thy crime. Thou knowest

that I do not fear solitude. And then I wish to reflect upon all that thou hast just told me."

Quickly the young man ran to his horse. With a bound he was in the saddle. And sending with his hand a kiss to Claire smilingly looking after him, he started with the impetuosity of a man who knows that she whom he loves is at the end of his road.

CHAPTER III.

ALONE, and absorbed in thought, Claire forgot the place where she was, forgot what was passing around her. A far-away tumult, accompanied by the flourish of the horn, ascended from the forest. Upon the paving-stones of the high-road, carriages were rolling sonorously. The young woman was blind and deaf to all that was not Philippe. She pleased herself by reconstructing her life as she would wish it to be, taking up again the current of the past and counting the days of happiness of which she had voluntarily deprived herself. Removed from that disastrous epoch, she could hardly understand the feelings that she had then obeyed. That sort of delirious pride to which she had fallen a prey was indeed inexplicable. That determination to be married before the Duke, seemed to her so pitiful that she reddened at it. Had she been so carried away by vulgar motives as to have compromised the whole of her life?

Claire told herself that Philippe, gravely outraged as he had been, could not show himself inexorable. She had, however, still before her eyes his profile severe and haughty. She had still in her ears the tone of his voice when he said : "You will one day learn the truth, you will know that you have been still more unjust than cruel, you may then kneel at my feet, imploring your pardon : I shall not have for you a word of pity."

This terrible speech, was it not dictated to him by anger? Was he a man to maintain it, without weakness and without forgiveness? She saw him again, his

forehead supported by his hands, crushed
by grief, then lifting up his head and
showing to her a face bathed in tears.
Certainly, he adored her, and that night
he would have given his life for a word
of hope, for a look of tenderness. Eight
months had since fled. Through the
cruel wound made by the hand of his
wife, had the love of Philippe quite passed
away ?

Claire, with the end of her foot, was
absently tracing some lines upon the
sand.

" When one has loved profoundly,"
said she aloud, as if she wished to put
the question that troubled her to the
woods, to the winds, to space, to the
whole of nature mysterious and absorbed,
that surrounded her, " when one has
loved as he loved me, is it possible to
forget ? "

"When one has loved profoundly," answered a mocking voice, which seemed to descend to her, "one never forgets."

Claire rose hastily, and, looking up, saw the Duke who, having entered the Kiosque a moment before, was smilingly regarding her and leaning his elbows on the balustrade.

"Own that I arrive just in time to answer you?" said he gaily. "Was it of me that you were thinking?"

Claire gazed at him, half closing her eyes with sovereign impertinence.

"*Ma foi*, no," replied she.

"So much the worse!"

"And you?" asked the young woman, "what do you come to seek here?"

The Duke descended the six steps of the perron, and approaching Claire:

"It is you that I seek," said he, bowing.

"With what intention?"

"With the intention of unbosoming myself to you. You received me badly enough an hour since, when I offered to you my company. I thought that you might perhaps have become more sociable. And I am here. Are you inclined to reply to me?"

"*Mon Dieu*, my dear Duke, I really think that we have nothing to say to each other."

"Are you sure of it? I aver with grief that you have become extremely deceitful. You have sorrow and you will not own it."

Claire disdainfully shrugged her shoulders:

"And I aver," said she, "that you have become intellectually lowered. You return incessantly to the same ideas, with a little wailing air that is displeasing. Reassure your too sensitive heart. I have no sorrows, and I am not disposed to have any in order to give you pleasure."

"Be it so!" replied the Duke with good humour. "I only ask to be mistaken. I have formed on the subject of yourself ideas which appear to me accurate. But we must believe, as you so kindly say, that I have lost my lucidity. This morning, it seemed to me that you were nervous, agitated. The chase was very attractive. You would not take part in it. You passed your time in observing your husband . . ."

"Well?" said Claire, repressing a movement.

"Well!" continued the Duke, "it is a singular thing, but M. Derblay had not at all the appearance of occupying himself with you. He was quite at the service of the Duchess who laid claim

to him as her cavalier. And you, instead
of being satisfied at seeing him gallantly
performing his duty, you darted at him
flashing glances."

" From which you have concluded ? "
asked Claire frigidly.

" That the good understanding you
pretend exists between you and himself
is not real, that he does not appreciate
at its value the treasure which chance,
or rather my ill-fortune, has given to
him. Then, how shall I say it to you?
A thousand little facts, formerly over-
looked, are grouped in my mind. I have
recalled the strange attitude you took
on the day of your marriage. I have
criticised your sadness, analyzed your
anger. And, having weighed the for and
the against, I have arrived at this conclu-
sion, that you have not, although you state
it, all the happiness that you deserve."

The attack was rude and direct. In a moment, the Duke had turned the defences so patiently raised by Claire. Audaciously, he gave her to understand that, like a fortress which has no exterior succour to expect, he was intending to make her undergo a regular siege. The young woman would not fall back a step; she even went to meet the attack, and, with a bitterness that she no longer concealed :

"Then, you, a compassionate and generous soul," said she, "you think that the moment is perhaps favourable to offer me some consolation?"

The Duke, with a wide experience of this little war, did not yet consent to follow Claire upon the ground that she so boldly offered to him. He would for ever have lost his cause by owning too promptly the calculation that he had

made. He wished to appear hurried
away by a feeling deep and serious.
And forsaking the tone of irony in which
he had hitherto spoken :

"You judge me unkindly, Claire," said
he with sadness ; "I have done, you may
indeed believe it, all that depended on me
to forget you. When I arrived here I
imagined that I loved you no longer. I
thought that I could see you again without
danger. The world said that you were
happy. And I was rejoiced at it. Ah !
poor fool that I was ! After so many
deceptions and ordeals, I believed my
heart worn out and dead. With a profound grief, I felt it become reanimated
and revived. In an instant I recovered
all my souvenirs. I saw you again, alas !
so troubled, notwithstanding the efforts
that you made, to dissemble your cares
and your sadness ! You would have

been able to deceive any other than myself. But for a long time your face has
known how to conceal nothing from my
eyes. Had you been happy, I should
have adored you from a distance, without
uttering a word to trouble your repose . . .
But you are suffering! Then, I am no
longer master of myself. I feel drawn
towards you by an irresistible power, and
I am confident that there is not for me,
in this world, any other woman than
yourself."

Claire heard with astonishment these
passionate words. Not a fibre of her
heart throbbed. That man, who was
speaking to her so tenderly, was it indeed
he whom she once loved to the degree of
nearly losing her reason for him? His
voice, that had formerly caused her to
thrill, left her now cold and a little irritated. She saw in him one of those

skilful actors able to shake the nerves and overturn the badly balanced minds of women. She did not think for a single instant that he could be sincere, and saw in his pursuit only the base desire to satisfy a sudden caprice.

"Do you know that you do not lack impudence?" said she with asperity. "Having had formerly to choose between a woman whom you professed to love, and a fortune that tempted you, you did not hesitate: but closed your heart and opened your cash-box. Now, to-day when you have money, you would not be sorry perhaps to have the woman also. And you come to make advances to me! Ah! my dear Duke, you are too ambitious! Not everything! That would be too much!"

The Duke shook his head with melancholy:

"How harshly you speak to me!" said

he. "I quite understand that you must always reproach me."

Claire made an abrupt movement, her eyes shone with indignation, and, in a peremptory voice:

"I reproach you!" cried she. "You flatter yourself, *mon cher!* If I have for you any feeling whatsoever, it is gratitude, for after all, if I am the wife of M. Derblay, who is as useful as you are useless, as unselfish as you are egotistic, as generous as you are despicable, in a word who has all the good qualities that you have not, and none of the defects that you possess, is it not to you that I owe it?"

The Duke bit his lips; each of the words of this violent apostrophe had struck him like a blow on the face.

"M. Derblay," said he, trying to subdue Claire with a look, "is without doubt perfect. But he has a slight defect which renders his perfection useless . . . to you, at least: he does not love you! A few months only has he been your husband. If he appreciated you at your true worth, he would be near you, attentive, and tender! Where is he? With the Duchess!"

"Your wife!" cried Claire with anger.

Then, making an effort over herself and regaining her calmness :

"Well! Why should I be affected by it, when it does not trouble you?"

"Oh! I am not jealous," replied the Duke in a light tone. "And then I am acquainted with the Duchess. She is an admirable doll, covered with lace and adorned with jewels. Under that attire, neither head nor heart. Where in her could passion find a lodging? Whilst your husband . . ."

He approached, and speaking close to the young woman, as if he feared that

the venom of his words, by passing
through the air, would lose its perfidious
sting :

" You saw him with her, only a moment
since . . . Oh ! The ingrate who disowns
his happiness ! The imprudent one who
risks to lose it ! Leave him with the
Duchess ; they are worthy of each other.
And suffer me to stay with you, I who
appreciate you, I who understand you, I
who love you ! "

Claire took a step back, as if to put a
greater distance between herself and the
Duke. Then, oppressed, wishing to appear
calm, and not succeeding :

" What you have just told me," said
she, " see, I laugh at it . . ."

" Yes, as *Figaro* says, so as not to be
obliged to weep at it," continued Bligny,
" for, in reality, it is profoundly sad.
You are united to a man who, for you,

will probably never be but a stranger.
Everything, in him and in you, is antago-
nistic. He is a plebeian and you are a
patrician. I am sure that he has prin-
ciples of equalization, and you, you are
aristocratic to the ends of your nails. He
is rough like all emanating from the
people, and that shocks you. You are
proud like all issuing from the nobility,
and that ruffles him. The two races from
which you spring are the born enemies
of each other. The forefathers of this
gentleman have very cheerfully cut off the
heads of your ancestors, *ma chère*. In a
word, everything disposes you to hate,
and nothing leads you to love each other."

Claire proudly raised her head, and
braving the Duke:

. "I love him, however," said she, "and
you know it!"

"You fancy that you love him!" continued Bligny with mildness, and as if trying to make a child hear reason, " Because you are jealous! But there are jealousies of all kinds. There is that which is born of love and there is also that which is born of pride. It is from the latter, I will swear it, that you are suffering. Your husband neglects you, and, little as you care for him, it irritates you. That is very natural! And you attach yourself to him from the spirit of contradiction. All women are thus constituted. The crisis through which you are passing, eh! *Mon Dieu*, I know it perfectly!"

Claire, silent, full of amazement and of disgust, heard the Duke develop his audacious analysis. Bligny took for curiosity that which was only stupor. And, eager to pursue the work of demoralization that he believed to have so well begun:

"Stay, I will play an open game with

you," added he, laughing, "cards upon the table ! The crisis is composed of four phases, like the motion of the moon. At this moment you are in the first, named the phase of resistance. Your husband escapes from you, and you are bent on re-conquering him : it is a fixed idea. He resists, and you will soon perceive that your efforts are useless. This gallant man, who limited himself to sentimentalizing, is marching resolutely to infidelity. And you will enter the second phase, that of lost illusions. All is crumbling, your illusions are lost, your tranquillity destroyed. You fall into profound dejection and you turn at first to God, the only consolator of great despairs. But, as your husband pursues the course of his successes, your faith begins to be embittered. That for-tunate man is too gay, and you are too sad. After all, you are only twenty-two

years old, and you have the right of love.
One cannot always live alone. A dull
irritation takes possession of you, and you
enter the third phase, that of anger. A
veil has fallen from your eyes, you see
your husband, such as he is in reality,
that is to say awkward, ordinary and
stupid. You are astonished at having re-
gretted him for a moment. And you dis-
cover in yourself vague aspirations towards
certain compensations. Ah! That time,
let the inconstant husband beware, for the
end of the crisis draws near! There you are,
blushing, but resolute, putting your pretty
foot into the phase of consolation. Look
before you; all is rose-coloured, all is
flowery, all is gay. In it one can forget
admirably! Now, yet another step and
you are there. You hesitate? Madame,
permit me to offer you my hand to do you
the honours of that phase, in which I await

you, with a little hope and an immensity of love."

The Duke wished to take the hand of Claire. Abruptly the young woman repulsed him, her face gloomy and menacing:

"Your calculations are ingenious," said she, "and testify to a long study of woman. Only I regret to see that if you have conscientiously observed the foolish and the depraved, you have neglected to take into account those who are honest. There are, I am proud to tell it to you, a few unhappy women who do not lose their reason, who refuse to avenge themselves, and find themselves sufficiently consoled by preserving their own self-respect and meriting the esteem of others."

"Well, well!" said the Duke, "you are in your part: the phase of resistance."

"If you persist, I shall but hate you!"

"I persist because I can but love you!"

"What you call your love is an unworthy persecution! What kind of man can you be thus to expose yourself to my hatred, after having deserved my contempt?"

The Duke remained an instant silent, gazing at Claire standing upright, shuddering and savage. A tress of her golden hair was loosened and floated glittering over her shoulder. Under her habit of blue cloth, her bosom was heaving, her hand, grasped her riding whip, agitating the slender toy of plaited leather like a weapon. She was admirable thus.

A mad passion seized de Bligny. He turned pale, his eyes became wild and troubled, and, walking towards the young woman, with open arms:

"Nothing will cost me too much to obtain you," stammered he.

He touched her. She felt his burning

breath pass over her face. She sprang back, her brows knit, her mouth contracted :

"Take care !" cried she : "if you make one step more, I will treat you as the worst of cowards, and lash you across the face !"

He saw her arm raised, energetic, formidable, ready to strike, and recoiled a step.

Then, proud at having triumphed, drawing up her tall figure, but yet trembling from the conflict :

"Have I, then, fallen so low that you dare thus to insult me ? Am I, then, so publicly forsaken that you can with impunity force me to undergo such outrages ? If I had near me a man to defend me, would you attack me in this manner ? But, I am alone, and you can permit yourself anything ! Well !

You see that I am capable of defending myself ! "

The Duke, again calm, bowed before the young woman.

" You will change," said he; " the future is mine. I am patient, I shall wait."

This cold and daring answer exasperated Claire. She regarded the Duke with angry eyes, and, her voice broken through the violence of her emotion :

" Know, then," cried she, " were I the most unhappy of women, were I—which is impossible—to become the most unworthy and to cast myself away ! Well ! You have inspired me with so much aversion and disgust, that I should take no matter whom, a stranger, a passer-by, rather than you ! "

This cry of rage left the Duke very cold. But, with the same confident smile that had the power of putting Claire beside herself, he said:

"We shall see!"   •

The young woman did not give herself the trouble to answer. She turned from him, and, walking towards the open space from which she was separated by a moving curtain of alders and aspens, approached the place where the footmen of M. Moulinet were preparing, for the huntsmen, an appetizing repast.

At the bottom of her heart, remained a feeling of fear caused by the rude aggression of the Duke. She had seen him, with eyes sparkling, with face pallid, with hands trembling, eager to seize her. She had a horror of the struggle from which, thanks to her energy, she had for once escaped. And having no longer confidence in the honour of this nobleman, whom she had during so long a time adored as a God, with an immense sadness, she went to place herself under the protection of the lackeys.

"Attention," said the chief *maître d'hôtel* to his assistants, "here are our people arriving."

By all the roads of the forest, like a roaring avalanche, the carriages were returning, rolling heavily over the green carpet of grass. The horsemen riding by the wings. And there was joyous conversation between these young people excited by a wild chase. They were still upwards of five hundred yards off and the sound of their animated voices was distinctly heard. Free from all cares, entirely given up to the sweetness of the present hour, they were enjoying to the utmost the beautiful day. Claire drew between that gaiety and her melancholy a sorrowful contrast. She reproached the whole of nature for being *en fête*, when she was so sad, not remembering, alas! that she herself was the sole author of her pain.

A carriage entering the Rond-point roused her from her distressing thoughts. The Marquise was seated in its depths, as in her vast easy-chair, a small lace shawl over her shoulders. Claire went to her as to her salvation. The air seemed purified by the presence of this noble woman, and, in a moment, she regained her tranquillity. Madame de Beaulieu, indolent as usual, had not hurried herself to drive to the forest. It was principally to see her daughter on horseback that she had torn herself from her gentle idleness, and had ordered horses to be put to her large chariot.

" What ?" said she, " thou art here,

quite alone ! Where, then, is thy husband ?
And Sophie, what is she doing ?"

" The Baroness has just left me,"
replied Claire without confusion ; " and, as
to Philippe, I insisted on his following the
hunt. A husband should not exhibit himself publicly with his wife, it provokes
gossip . . ."

She was laughing and placid. The
Marquise contemplated her with deep
satisfaction. Never had a suspicion
touched her rather superficial mind.

" You are so happy that you can give
yourself the luxury of hiding your happiness," said Madame de Beaulieu. " Ah !
Philippe is the pearl of sons-in-law ! . . ."

The ruck of the horsemen, arriving at a
quick trot, cut short the words of the
Marquise, and permitted Claire to dissemble the embarrassment caused to her
by the eulogies of her mother. La Brède

and du Tremblaye, upon their horses white with foam, the one crimson as if on the point of apoplexy, the other very pale and seeming ready to faint, were noisily surrounded by the joyous squadron, lavishly scattering words of praise upon the vigour with which the two young men had supported the pursuit. Pontac, his horn *à la Dampierre* at his mouth, was sounding with the full power of his lungs the *Hallali,* while the *piqueur* Bistocq, on foot, with arms swinging, rounding his back with a sulky air, his face red, and dragging after him his tall, raw-boned horse, was mumbling between his teeth violent criticisms, directed at amateurs " who played at hunting, breaking the backs of brave good horses, to run after pieces of paper, saving your presence, as if they were *chiffoniers !* "

With a quick glance, Claire saw

Philippe who was riding with Suzanne
and the Baroness. Sophie, being first,
stopped near her friend and whispered
in her ear these words, which brought
roses to the cheeks of the young
woman :

" When we overtook them, he was
no longer with Athénaïs. He had
forsaken her very cleverly, leaving her
to that idiot de Pontac, who only
knows how to make a noise with his
hunting-horn. A pretty talent that of
his, the great booby ! And agreeable in
society ! "

She began to laugh, regarding, while
half closing her eyes, with the involuntary
insolence of the short-sighted, Athénaïs,
who was arriving deafened by the horn of
her companion, but not daring to speak,
from the dread of appearing to fail in good
breeding.

However, on perceiving Claire, Athénaïs started her horse at a gallop, and ad-dressing an ironical gesture to the Duke, standing motionless and indifferent, a few paces from the carriage of Madame de Beaulieu :

" Well ! Duke, here you are, found again ? At the same time as Madame Derblay, eh ? It is very amiable of you to have remained to keep your cousin company ! "

Athénaïs darted a diabolical glance at Philippe, trying to make her injurious thought penetrate into his mind. She wished in this manner to take her revenge for the rather humiliating way in which he had so promptly left her. The Iron-master, having taken a resolution, stepped forward firm and almost menacing. Claire turned pale. Were these two men to be brought into collision with each other through the implacable hatred of the Duchess ?

" I have not been so fortunate as to be able to keep my cousin company, as you so elegantly express yourself," replied the Duke bowing respectfully before Madame Derblay. " When I arrived here, my aunt had anticipated me."

" Then, *mon cher*, it is that you have a bad horse, you must change him," rejoined the Duchess.

And, her teeth clenched by anger at seeing her malice thwarted, she gave a violent stroke with her whip over the ears of her mare, who bounded aside and reared, furiously shaking her bits white with foam.

The Duke advanced coldly, seized the animal by the bridle, drew her down to the ground, and, assisting Athénaïs to dismount :

"Nothing is in worse taste than to punish in that way your horse, *ma chère*," said he, with his impertinent manner. "Without taking into consideration that you ride indifferently, and that you might get yourself thrown . . . which would have a bad appearance. Believe me, get rid of those habits : they smell too strongly of the shop !"

And leaving the Duchess pallid from rage, with his usual tranquil gait, Bligny went to join his friends and to toast with them the success of the day.

Claire, shivering and cold, stepped into the carriage with her mother, and begged to be taken back to Pont-Avesnes. She had a weight upon her heart. The answer given by the Duke to Athénaïs, which had so opportunely prevented the dangerous intervention of Philippe, appeared to Claire to have made her his accomplice.

She was upon the point of telling everything to her husband, preferring his cen-
sure, his anger, to that odious connivance
with the man who had insulted her. But
she feared to speak. And sighing, she
saw herself condemned eternally to this
falsehood, which caused her so violent a
repulsion, obliged to deceive, everywhere
and always, and to show a smiling face
with despair in her soul.

She cast timid glances upon Philippe,
who was riding beside Bachelin again
seated in his cabriolet. The Ironmaster
showed a tranquil face. He was conversing with the old Notary, his voice
betraying no emotion. Claire thought
that she had deceived herself, in fancying
that she saw a gleam of anger in his
eyes, when he was advancing towards
the Duke. But she was acquainted
with the power that Philippe had over

himself. Perhaps, at this moment, he
was constraining himself to appear careless.

Claire hoped that he was jealous. At
the risk of her life, she desired to see him
led away into threatening her, raising his
hand against her, as he had once done on
that terrible night. She could not consent to remain longer in uncertainty. She
promised herself to speak to him the next
day for her brother, and to penetrate at
last into the mysterious mind of her husband. Her resolution taken, Claire wished
to be gay, she made an effort to dissipate
the cloud which shadowed her forehead,
and, like an actor who steps upon the
stage to play his part, she masked her
face in smiles.

In the distance, under the trees, they
heard the far-away murmur of the
joyous company, and, awaking the echoes

of the woods, the horn of Pontac who was sounding the death of the stag, represented in the dissimilar persons of the big La Brède and of the little du Tremblaye.

———

CHAPTER IV.

IN his large study with severe furniture,
Philippe had disposed himself to work.
His bureau was covered with papers, over
which he cast a rapid glance. With a
stroke of his pen, he affixed his signature
to the document examined, and quickly,
without hesitation, he passed to another.
It was ten o'clock. The burning sun beat
perpendicularly upon the façade of the
Château. An indiscreet ray strayed
through the window, and, glancing upon
the forehead of the Ironmaster, interrupted his work. He rose, and, going to
the window, allowed his eyes to wander
over the garden.

At the margin of the little lake,

sheltered under a tent of striped canvas, Suzanne, wearing a white gown, was absently fishing. Her line immersed in the basin, and her float, agitated by the pulling of a fish which had seized the bait, bobbed up and down, making the water ripple in sparkling circles. The young girl, her eyes, gazing into space, seemed to follow with satisfaction a happy thought. She stood motionless, her face radiant, lost in a dream.

A smile passed over the lips of Philippe. He gently opened his window, and, speaking to the young girl :

" Suzanne," said he, " thou hast a bite ! "

. She started, and turning towards her brother with a playful face :

" Oh, Philippe ! " exclaimed she, " thou didst frighten me ! "

" Draw in thy line," said the Ironmaster; "for ten minutes a perch has been floundering at the end. It is not well to make creatures suffer thus! . . ."

Instinctively Suzanne lifted the slender rod, the flexible end of which caused the fish to spring from the water, like a flash of silver. The young girl, with her gloved hand, unhooked the perch and dropped it into a string bag lying in the water under the grass of the bank.

"I have twelve," cried Suzanne proudly, showing to her brother her full bag.

"That will make a dish," said the Ironmaster gaily. "They must have bitten eagerly!"

He watched for a moment his little sister, who was gravely baiting her hook. Under the blue sky, in the imperfect shadow of the tent, she appeared so rosy, so youthful, that sudden compassion seized upon her brother. A sigh swelled his chest; he sent to the adored child a silent kiss. And, letting fall the blind which secured him from the sun, he re-closed his window. The study was plunged in a cool half obscurity. Derblay, returning to his bureau, was about to seat himself, when a tap lightly struck upon the door arrested him.

"Come in," said he with indifference.

The door opened, and Claire, blushing, very agitated, but determined, appeared upon the threshold.

"I shall not disturb you?" asked she, approaching, while Philippe, much surprised at this unexpected visit, courteously drew forward an arm-chair.

"Not the least in the world," replied he, simply. And, leaning against the chimney-piece, he waited.

Claire sat down, her head a little supported upon the back of her chair, and gazed for an instant around her. She had never before entered this room which was altogether personal to Philippe. Its gravity a little cold, like a reflection of the character of him who inhabited it, pleased her. She examined every object with attention. In reality, she was not sorry to delay the moment when it would be necessary to speak. Her heart was beating very fast, and her temples were throbbing.

Philippe standing, and upon his guard, observed her. It was he who, first, broke the silence.

"Have you something to ask me?" said he.

Claire turned her eyes towards her husband, and with a shade of sadness in her voice:

"We are living so estranged from each other, that I must have a request to address to you, before I can risk disturbing you."

Philippe made a gesture of polite denial, and bowing before his wife, as if to encourage her:

"I am listening to you."

The young woman bent her head, as if wishing to collect her thoughts. She trembled, and her lips were dry. Never was a more serious game engaged in with greater anguish.

"That which I have to name to you," said she, "is of the utmost importance, and interests you at least as much as myself."

"Let me hear it."

Claire cast at her husband a glance so charged with dumb prayers, that he ought to have fallen at her feet. He remained circumspect, waiting.

"But, first of all," continued the young woman, "tell me, you take some interest in Octave, do you not?"

"I do not think," said the Ironmaster, rather astonished, "that your brother has had cause to question it."

The answer was ambiguous. Claire slightly frowned.

"If you had the opportunity of proving to him that interest?"

"It is probable that I should seize it."

It was to this precise point that Claire had wished to lead her husband, setting for him a snare by her questions. There was only to indicate to him the object of this conversation. Carried on by the heat of the struggle begun, she hesitated no longer.

"Well," said she, "that opportunity has presented itself. Do you desire to know it? I ought to tell you that it is of importance, and that on this occasion it is not only a question of my brother . . ."

"How you beat about the bush!" interrupted the Ironmaster. "What you have to ask of me, does it appear to you so difficult to obtain ? "

Claire looked her husband straight in the face, as if she did not wish to lose the slightest change of expression, then, courageously :

" Judge of it yourself," said she. " Octave loves your sister, and has commissioned me to ask her of you for him."

Philippe let fall a pained exclamation. His face became gloomy. To conceal his trouble, he took several steps towards the window, before which he stood silent, lifting with his hand the light window-blind. At the edge of the sheet of water, Suzanne, unconscious of all that was passing, continued to dream, allowing her line to float in the mirror-like water. The Ironmaster regarded the frank and gentle girl. She was made for happiness.

Claire, devoured by anxiety, went up to her husband and, seeing him pensive and absorbed:

"You do not answer?" said she.

Philippe turned and, speaking slowly, as if his words cost him much:

"I am grieved for your brother, but this marriage is impossible."

"You refuse?" cried Claire, a prey to terrible trouble.

"I refuse," repeated the Ironmaster coldly.

"Wherefore?"

Philippe gazed fixedly at his wife as if he wished his answer to penetrate to the bottom of her heart:

"Because there is already," said he, "one unhappy person in my family, made so by yours, and I find that one is sufficient!"

"Take care," rejoined Claire quickly,

"not to cause more certainly the un-happiness of Suzanne by refusing her to my brother."

" How so ? " said the Ironmaster with sudden animation.

" She loves him."

In the garden, the joyous voice of Suzanne, setting in order, with the assist-ance of Brigitte, her fishing-tackle, made itself heard.

Philippe paused for an instant to listen to her.

" She loves him," repeated he. " That is indeed a great misfortune. But it will not change my decision. If, on the eve of the day when I was about to marry you, some one had prevented me from doing so, and had set me free though with my heart broken, he would have rendered me an immense service. The cruel ex-perience that I have undergone, at least will have served some purpose. If my sister must weep, she shall weep at liberty, and she shall not, like myself, see before her, a future irremediably lost."

Claire was so sharply attacked that she could not preserve her coolness.

"It is revenge that you are seeking!" said she with violence.

"Revenge!" said the Ironmaster haughtily. "Do you believe that it suits me to accept it? No! It is a precaution that I am taking, and everything advises it."

Claire sank into her arm-chair. She felt in the words of her husband such disdain and such determination that she renounced fighting, and only thought of imploring.

"See," said she, "I pray you, do not render me responsible for the unhappiness of these children . . . It is enough that

I should suffer. What must I do to prevail on you! I was very wrong with regard to you, I know it . . ."

Philippe began to laugh bitterly :

" You were very wrong with regard to me ? " said he; " truly ? And you deign to own it ? But these are, it seems to me, great concessions that you are making ! "

Claire did not notice the ironical words of her husband; she was determined to let nothing dishearten her, and to persevere to the end :

" Yes, I have wronged you greatly," replied she, " but you are making me expiate it very cruelly . . ."

" I ? " interrupted Philippe. " And how ? Have I addressed to you a single reproach ? Have I ever said to you a wounding word ? Have I failed in consideration towards you ? "

" No ! But how much I should have

preferred your anger to the haughty
indifference with which you treat me.
Around me I hear everyone extolling my
happiness. Wherever I go they envy me,
they *fête* me. I return to our home.
Where is my happiness? I seek it, and
I find only solitude, desertion, sadness."

Philippe drew up his tall figure, and
subjugating the poor woman whom he
felt to have fallen so completely into his
power :

"It does not rest with me," said he,
"that it is so. You have yourself determined your life. It is such as you chose
to make it."

"It is true," replied Claire in a broken
voice, "but at least I had a right to
expect tranquillity, and I am not even
able to obtain that . . ."

She rose, her hands clenched, distracted
and moaning :

" The wicked woman who hates me, comes here to pursue me, and you tolerate it, you lend yourself to her plots and schemes ! . . . She parades you, she compromises you ! And you have not for me so much pity as to spare me her outrageous bravado ! . . . Oh ! But I am at the end of my patience, it cannot last much longer, I will not have it ! "

" You will not have it ? " repeated Philippe.

And as Claire again said with mad obstinacy :

" No ! No ! I will not have it ! "

" You forget," said the Ironmaster severely, " that here there is only myself who has the right to say : I will ! "

All the blood of the proud young woman rushed to her face. She rebelled, and blinded by anger, hurried away by jealousy :

" Beware ! " cried she. " Do not drive me too far ! . . . I can bear your indifference, but a disdain so insulting, a desertion so public . . . I will never submit to it ! "

Philippe paused before her, and, regarding her with mocking curiosity :

"It is indeed yourself!" said he: "you have remained just the same! Always proud! You are disquieting yourself as to what your neighbours may think. Public opinion, this is what occupies you above everything. It was to make a good figure in the eyes of the world that you threw yourself like a madwoman into the adventure of our marriage. And to-day even, exasperated at the thought that people may criticise you, may laugh at you, you lose all restraint, you forget yourself so far as to threaten me ! "

"Oh! No! I do not threaten," interrupted Claire, no longer able to suppress her tears, "I implore. Have pity on me, Philippe. Be generous . . . Will you never be tired of striking so cruelly upon my heart? You are indeed avenged, you can afford to be indulgent . . . If you will alter nothing in the conditions of our existence, at least assure to me tranquillity, deliver me from the Duchess . . . Remove from me the Duke . . ."

She pronounced these last words in a low voice, as if she were ashamed of letting them fall from her lips . . .

"Of what do you complain?" rejoined the Ironmaster. "I tolerate them myself, the Duke and Duchess . . . They are your relations! What would the world say, that world to the opinion of which you subordinate everything, if, without reason, we close our doors against them? We must wait patiently and submit to the exigencies of our sad condition. Life does not modify itself, at the will or caprice of a spoiled child. All in it is grave and serious. And misfortune comes but too easily. It is not necessary to go to meet her. You know it now. Both thrown, by you, out of the beaten track, our duty is to walk straight on, as we have not the power of turning back."

"Then," said Claire, "I have nothing to expect from you, nothing to hope?"

"Nothing!" said Philippe coldly. "And remember that it is you who would have it so."

Claire looked at her husband. The features of the Ironmaster were changed. His eyes had sunk under their lids. He was pale, but his voice was firm.

She had a momentary thought of casting herself at his feet, of opening to him her heart, of owning to him that she loved him. She walked towards him. vaguely stretching out her hands, her bosom oppressed, suffocating . . . But a last remnant of pride stopped her, and sighing profoundly, she remained motionless.

Philippe came to her.

"I am obliged to go to the foundry," said he, calmly, as if nothing had passed between himself and that woman whom he adored. "Excuse me for leaving you."

"What shall I reply to my brother?" asked Claire timidly.

"Tell him that I rely upon his loyalty not to say a single word of my refusal to Suzanne. I shall make arrangements in the next eight days, to send away for a time that child."

And passing like a shadow through the dimly lighted study, he gave to Claire a little nod full of indifference and went out.

The young woman was during some moments alone in the vast room. She abandoned herself to her grief, without restraint. Lying back upon the divan, she weighed the extent of her misfortune. Thus, it was irrevocable. Vainly had she disclosed to Philippe the bleeding wound in her heart : he merely cast upon it an absent glance. She existed no more for him. He had said it to her, and he kept his promise. Implacable, he would not forgive her transient alienation. He repulsed her when she went to him. She accused herself of having spoiled the future of her brother. It was through distrust of the de Beaulieu blood, of which he had proved the fatal violence, that the Ironmaster refused Suzanne to Octave. How was she to tell him the distressing news ?

The voice of Suzanne sounding in the adjoining room made her rise to her feet, with the rapidity of a roe-deer which hears the baying of the hounds, she feared to be surprised weeping alone in the study of her husband, and ran to shut herself into her room. She sent word, at the hour of the second breakfast, that she was suffering and could not go down. Then, towards two o'clock, when from her window she had seen Suzanne bury herself in the umbrageous clumps of trees of the Park, she furtively gained the staircase, and, through the little gate of the court, started on foot for Beaulieu.

The Marquis, impatient to learn the result of the negotiation engaged in by his sister, had walked a thousand times up and down the terrace, being quite certain that the young woman would not leave him long in suspense. In the distance, he saw Claire ascending the rather steep road which led to the Château. He was painfully struck by her carriage. Madame Derblay was slowly following the · grassy slope, her head bent, forgetting to shelter herself, although the sun, gleaming now and then from behind the clouds, was very powerful. Her step, · languid and reluctant, announced defeat. She was not coming triumphant and alert like a messenger of good tidings.

In an instant, the young man reached Claire. They exchanged a glance. That of the brother anxious and troubled, that of the sister gloomy and hopeless.

"*Mon Dieu*, what has happened?"

murmured Octave seizing Claire convulsively by the arm, and drawing her
towards a small open space surrounded
by benches, from which there was a lovely
view. An exquisite odour of lime-trees in
blossom, borne to Claire, ended by un-
nerving her, and trembling, her eyes full
of tears, she stood before her brother
without articulating a word.

"Now, Claire, for pity's sake," exclaimed the Marquis, "what ails thee?
Speak, anything is better than thy
silence."

Madame Derblay had compassion for the
anxiety of her brother, and, making a
painful effort:

"I have, my poor boy, a sorrowful
answer to make to the request with which
thou didst charge me," said she. "A
marriage between Suzanne and thee is
impossible."

Octave recoiled a step, as if he had seen a gulf open at his feet. He looked at his sister with amazement, not quite understanding, and repeated :

"Is impossible? . . . How? . . . "

Claire shook her head dejectedly :

"Philippe has refused," said she.

"What reason did thy husband give?" asked the Marquis.

Claire remained dumb. Her embarrassment was extreme. What could she say to her brother? Could she reveal to him the secret of her grievous existence? What pretext could she invent to give to the refusal of Philippe a rational meaning? And she must answer, without appearing to hesitate. Octave was fixing his sister with his eyes, seeking the truth in her face, and in her slightest gesture.

"He did not give the reason," stammered Claire reddening from shame, "he refused to explain himself."

"Without any reason?" said the Marquis filled with astonishment, "without explanation? He, Philippe, whom I like so much! He has not hesitated to cause me such grief?"

Greatly moved, Octave hastily wiped his eyes, and his active brain pursuing the motive that Philippe had not wished to give, and which escaped him, seated himself in silence, seeking, desperately . . . Suddenly he gave a cry: a ray of light illumined his mind. Money! . . . It could only be money. He was without fortune and without position. That was surely the reason for which Philippe refused to him Suzanne. He rose quickly.

Claire regarded him with disquietude. The Marquis took several hasty steps, and, speaking aloud, answering his thought, without being aware of it, his face radiant with confidence and with ardour :

"Without position, it is true, but I will make one," said he. "Without fortune . . . Well! Philippe knows how one can grow rich . . . I will do as he . . ."

He stopped, stupefied, almost appalled. Claire had sprung up, seizing his hand with force. One word had struck her, one only, in all that her brother had said : "Without fortune!" But it sufficed to throw her into inexpressible agitation. And, forgetting his preoccupations, his cares, his griefs, with the whole strength of her being, she wished Octave to explain himself.

"Without fortune, thou?" repeated she.

And, with an imperious gesture, menacing even, she claimed an answer.

Octave, embarrassed, confused, attempted to put her off. But with a terrible violence, suspecting a mystery that she must at any cost clear up, Claire took him by the shoulder, and devouring him with her eyes :

" What didst thou say ? "

" I imprudently let fall," replied Octave, " some words that thou shouldst never have heard . . . Thou art ignorant of the loss of our law-suit. Thou shouldst have ignored it always . . . And I, simpleton that I am, I have betrayed the secret that I promised to keep ! "

But Claire was no longer listening to the Marquis: she was thinking. The law-suit lost, it was ruin. Her brother without fortune, herself without dowry. A horrible doubt seized her: she shuddered, her eyes grew large, and, turning to Octave :

" When I was married ? . . ." said she
only, ending her phrase by a gesture.

" The disaster was accomplished."

" And my husband . . . Philippe ? Did
he know it ?"

" He knew it. And he prohibited us
from speaking of it to thee. He would
not see a shadow upon thy brow. He
showed on that occasion unparalleled
generosity and delicacy . . ."

Claire gave a cry of anguish, and beating the air with her hands, like a madwoman, her voice broken :

" He has done that !" cried she, " and
I ! . . . I ! Oh ! unhappy that I am !"

In a sudden rush of memory, the room
hung with tapestry, upon which the warriors were silently smiling at the goddesses, appeared to her, such as it was on
the night of her marriage, with the large
fire burning on the hearth, against the

chimney-piece of which she had shudder-
ingly leaned. She recalled Philippe, pale
and trembling, almost at her feet, then
proudly raising his head when she had
said to him: "Take my fortune! , . ."
Her fortune! How he had smiled with
disdain! She now understood wherefore.
And in her despair the truth, so heart-
rending and so humiliating, rose to her
lips. She must speak, she must accuse
herself. Frantic, and seized with a furious
desire to punish her body, not being able
to punish her soul:

"Oh! I lied to thee just now," stammered she, "when I told thee that I did
not know why he had refused thee his
sister. It is on account of me, unworthy
creature that I am, the cause of misfortune
to all who approach me!"

And, with an outburst, she made to her
brother her sad confession, extenuating

nothing, dwelling upon her injustice, and showing in all its horror the deed that she had committed.

"And he," continued she, "so proud, so disinterested, so good, even in his anger, for he spared me ! With a word he could have crushed me. He did not do it ! And I,—I heard him imploring me. I saw him weeping, and I remained insensible. I did not understand all that there was in his heart of deep and sincere love ! "

Then, transformed by grief, radiant from passion :

" But if thou hadst not spoken, wicked one, my life would have been for ever lost ! What should I have become ? And it was by chance that thou didst tell me all ! Oh ! blessed be thou ! "

She caught her brother in her arms and embraced him with desperate thankfulness.

And words, like a wave too long checked, flowed from her lips.

"Claire, calm thyself, I pray thee!" said Octave, terrified.

"Fear nothing, all is now saved," continued she, in a state of exaltation, "I will repair the evil that I have done, I shall insure thy happiness . . . Philippe! Oh! I will throw myself at his feet. All will be easy and sweet to me so that I succeed . . . I was again to-day very indiscreet when speaking with him. But I was not mistress of myself, thou seest! I love him so much!"

A cloud passed over her face. The disquieting recollection of the Duchess returned to her. She knit her brows, and with a hollow voice:

"Oh! I will not let her take him from me now! He must come back to me, or I shall die!"

" Claire ! " exclaimed the Marquis.

But with extreme mobility, she had, from sadness, passed to joy. And her face grew calm.

"Have no fear," continued she, laughing gaily. "We receive to-morrow, it is my *fête* . . . All our friends will be there . . . I will be beautiful and please him . . . I shall triumph, I am sure of it ! And I shall again see him near me, confiding and tender . . . "

Her nerves, which alone had sustained her, suddenly gave way. She wavered and fell into the arms of Octave, who carried her to the grassy bank. Heart-rending sobs burst from her bosom. And for a long time she was overwhelmed with grief, hearing, without speaking, . the affectionate consolations of her brother.

When she had regained her self-possession, she remained grave, seated near the Marquis, gazing at the valley spread out before her, green and placid, traversed by the Avesnes winding through the fields like a silver ribbon. The park extended to the foot of the hills, the dark clumps of its tall trees surmounted by the pointed roofs of the Château. The lofty chimneys of the Foundry threw across the sky their heavy smoke, and the steeple of the little church rose, crowned by its weather-cock, which glittered in the oblique rays of the setting sun.

It was in this tranquil spot that Claire dreamed of living. She remembered that formerly, from that same place, she had regarded it with disdain and anger. Now, to her, it represented Paradise. Philippe was there.

CHAPTER V.

THE *fête* of *Sainte-Claire* had fallen this year upon a Sunday. The *fête* of *Sainte-Suzanne,* by a happy coincidence, was the preceding day. Philippe who, since the shipwreck of his happiness, subordinated all his actions to the necessities of his position, had not believed it possible to exempt himself from celebrating this double anniversary. He had not received since his marriage. The illness of Claire had lasted throughout the winter, and her convalescence was prolonged so far into the spring that the Ironmaster could, in the eyes even of the most suspicious, be excused for having kept his doors closed.

The mental agitation of Claire having, at different times, betrayed itself rather visibly, the Ironmaster resolved to make a public show of his tenderness for his wife, by giving a *fête* in her honour. For ten days the invitations had been issued when the attempt at a reconciliation, made by the young woman, brought the painful condition of things which existed between them from a chronic to an acute state.

Philippe, discouraged, thought for a moment of putting off his guests. But as it was the eve of the chosen day, he relied upon the energy of Claire; knowing that, from pride, she was capable of showing an unclouded brow to all her surroundings. And his heart lacerated, discontented with others and with himself, the Ironmaster prepared on his side to do gaily the honours of Pont-Avesnes.

Shut up, since the morning, in her

apartment, with the Baroness, Claire was
making ready for the conflict. She wished
to please, and was lying in a half light,
reposing herself so as to have a good
complexion. She dressed herself with as
much care as a courtezan who wishes to
make the conquest of a Nabob, neglecting
none of the artifices of the *toilette*, and
heightening, by the charm of apparel, her
incomparable beauty.

She had selected a white robe, trimmed
with Valenciennes and ornamented with
bouquets of natural roses. The bodice
cut low in the back, allowed to be seen,
her magnificent shoulders, and rather *dé-
colleté* in front, showed her superb bust,
the whiteness of which was further increased
by the bright colour of a garland of roses,
fastened to the narrow sleeve, and falling
to the bottom of the skirt, wreathing the
young woman in its perfumed sprays.

Her beautiful golden hair was gathered in a mass on the top of her head, boldly revealing the snowy nape of her neck, and bore for its sole ornament a cluster of *roses du Roi.* She was so beautiful thus, that Brigitte and Suzanne, who had themselves dressed her, seized with admiration, began to clap their hands. Claire cast a thankful look at the glass, and, trembling, the hour having come to appear, she descended.

In the large Louis XIV. salon, Philippe, in a black coat and white cravat, and the Baron, the sleeves of his jacket turned up and his hands quite yellow, were talking under the light of the burning chandelier. The Baroness, who entered with Claire, gave an exclamation of despair.

"Ah! *Mon ami,* from whence have you come, in that state and at such an hour? And what hands you have!"

" Pardon me, *chère amie*," said the Baron, reddening like a schoolboy caught in a fault, " I was a little delayed at the laboratory . . . And it is a bath of iodine, that I overturned by inadvertence, which has slightly discoloured my fingers . . ."

" Slightly ! " cried the young woman, " it is horrible, you will not be presentable . . . You look like a photographer ! . . ."

The Baron began to laugh :

" That would do well, I assure you."

And he went towards his wife.

" Do not come near me ! " said she, drawing back with consternation : " I have a new robe ! Quick, go to dress yourself. You have just time ! "

The Baron, delighted to get off so easily, disappeared with the celerity of a sylph.

Philippe gazed at Claire. In all the

splendour of her beauty, she was advancing towards him. She was radiant, and no trace of her cares could be seen upon her face. The Ironmaster admired the strength of soul of his wife. He thought that she was indeed courageous, and was thankful to her for performing so brilliantly her duty. Addressing to her a smile that made her pale with joy, he approached her, holding in his hand a casket of black leather upon which the initials C. D. were engraved.

"You are not rich in jewels," said he bowing before her. "At the time of our marriage, I was not able to procure for you all that I desired. Let me now repair that omission."

And he offered to her the casket. Claire, disconcerted, hesitated to take it. The Baroness seized it eagerly, opened it, and, drawing from it a marvellous *rivière* in diamonds, with cries of joy, she made it sparkle in the light:

"Oh! *Ma chère,* see, it is a princely present!"

The face of Claire darkened. It was indeed a princely present. She thought of the forty thousand francs, the pretended interest of her dowry, which were lying in a drawer of her handsome ebony cabinet. She added them to the enormous sum that the necklace must have cost, and felt humiliated to the depths of her soul. What a lesson in generosity Philippe was again giving to her! Money, that had been her supreme argument, he dispensed with a royal indifference, seeming to think it of no importance, although he had gained it by hard work.

"Now, Philippe, you must yourself fasten on her throat this token of bond-

age. It is indeed the least that you
can do," said the Baroness maliciously.

Then, turning to her husband who
was entering, clothed with perfect correctness :

"You who are always seeking little
pebbles, *mon cher*, try to find something
of this kind ! "

The Ironmaster fastened with a trembling hand the ribbon of silver, adorned
by glorious gems, upon the throat of his
wife. He brushed lightly with his fingers
that skin of creamy satin, and saw her
shiver at his touch.

"Now ! Now ! " exclaimed the Baroness, "on a day like this, it is the rule,
you must embrace her . . ."

And she shoved Claire into the arms of
Philippe who became pale as death. The
Ironmaster touched with his lips the
forehead of his wife, and, his throat

contracted by emotion, his eyes troubled, asking himself with anguish if he was about to swoon, he took the most cold and the most coveted of kisses.

Then, abruptly, he passed into the adjoining salon, eager to tear himself from the seductive sweetness of this proximity.

Claire had not till this time been able to realize thoroughly the importance of her husband's position. Wherever he went, she saw him received with deference and *empressement.* It was by entertaining at her house all the considerable people of the department that she discovered what influence the Ironmaster possessed.

The dinner brought together, M. Monicaud, the metamorphosed Republican Préfet, knowing how to soften his opinions when in society; the Procureur Général, a man grave and starched; the Trésorier-

Payeur, formerly a free-liver, very amiable, and the General Commanding the Division. All the civil and military authorities. The Metropolitan of Besançon, Monseigneur Fargis, to whom Philippe had presented a beautiful screen for the choir of the Cathedral, had consented to leave home, which he seldom did for any one. And, seated at the right of Claire, this smiling old man, with charming grace, braved the presence of M. le Préfet du Doubs who had implacably executed the Decrees.

Athénaïs, consumed by envy, assisted at the triumph of her rival. Claire, supported, for the first time, by the glance of her husband, regained her confidence. She conversed with spirit, finding the exact subject with which to flatter the self-love of each of her guests. Feeling herself admired by Philippe, and devoured by the desire to please him, she displayed all the resources of a superior mind.

The Duke was struck by her radiant brilliancy. The young woman, straining every nerve to charm, was indeed dazzling. Bligny, fascinated, allowed himself to contemplate her with an admiration that he did not attempt to conceal. His eyes fixed upon her, he forgot those who surrounded him. His passion, stimulated, made him lose all control. He did not see Philippe who was observing him with menacing attention. Besides, of what consequence was a husband to him? The world had long known, that Bligny would not hesitate to take the life of the husband after having taken his honour.

Moulinet, although he was much engaged in beguiling the Préfet, who gave

himself up,—with an abandonment full
of revelation as to his past life rich
in privations,—to the enjoyment of the
good cheer, was impressed by the manner
of Bligny. He had not refrained from
remarking that the Duke, since his
return, occupied himself a great deal
too much with Claire. He usually attached no importance to these senti-
mentalities of the young man. But, in
this special case, he was keenly disquieted.
The Ironmaster was a power, and, on the
eve of the elections, it was necessary to
treat him with caution. He promised
himself to remonstrate with his son-in-
law.

The Duchess, placed near Philippe,
endeavoured by her prattle to attract
his attention. She found him absent,
cold, preoccupied. The Marquise de
Beaulieu, seated at the right of the Iron-

master, was much tormented by the heat
of the lustres, and with her fan tried to
protect her forehead. Philippe, obliged
to be courteous to the right and to the
left and to be at the disposition of everyone, suffered horribly at seeing the Duke
gazing at Claire. It seemed to him
that the eyes of Bligny, wandering over
the bare shoulders of the young woman,
sullied them by visionary caresses. A
terrible anger took possession of him. He
understood all the torments of jealousy.
And he dreamed of the deep delight of
killing this man who, having already
done him so much harm, was still tor-
turing him so cruelly.

The frivolous words of Athénaïs, burning to monopolize him before the eyes of
all, fatigued him. And he ardently wished
to be delivered from these two odious
beings. The recollection of the prayer of

his wife, begging him to remove from her
the Duke and the Duchess, returned to him.
He comprehended the weariness of Claire,
exposed to the hatred of the wife and to
the love of the husband, and resolved to
free her from both. But to banish the
Duke, would no longer be sufficient. He
hated him too much.

The end of dinner was a relief to him.
Upon the terrace it was deliciously cool.
A charming surprise awaited Claire there.
The clumps of trees in the park were
illumined, and garlands of flowers were
wreathed over the whole façade of the
Château.

Moulinet had pillaged his hot-houses for
the occasion, and a flat basket, three
yards wide, in osiers woven and gilded,
was filled with the most admirable
orchids.

"My gardener tore out his hair on

seeing it leave La Varenne," said with an indifferent air, half contemptuously, the late Judge at the Tribunal de Commerce, to those who complimented him.

Nevertheless he did not lose sight of his son-in-law who had succeeded, by manœuvring with skill, in separating Claire from the group of young women, and imprisoning her in a convenient corner.

There, these two who had loved each other, were smilingly exchanging the most dangerous words. The Duke, impassioned, eager to conciliate the good graces of the young woman, was eulogizing her beauty and protesting his love, Claire, ungovernable, violent, wishing to escape from a *tête-à-tête* which caused her disgust, was raising by degrees her voice at the risk of attracting the attention of Philippe.

Then Bligny changed his tactics : he became mild and honied ; and spoke but of friendship. He asked Claire only to give him her hand, in token of pardon. And, while saying these words, his eyes, giving the lie to his language, blazed, full of passion. He drew near her little by little. One moment, emboldened by the half obscurity, he pressed so closely against her that she exclaimed :

"Take care ! If you do not go away, even at the risk of a scandal, I will call my husband !"

The Duke had raised the excitement of the young woman to an extreme point. It was Moulinet who saved, for the moment, the situation. He came, smilingly, to put himself as a third person between Bligny and Claire, entering into conversation through one of those common-places, in which he excelled, and which wonderfully provoked his son-in-law :

"How clear is the sky!" said the late Judge at the Tribunal de Commerce, with an elegiac air. "The moon is in her first quarter. It will be fine the whole week!"

The Duke regarded Moulinet askance, Claire, profiting by the diversion, escaped quickly. Bligny took a step to follow her. His father-in-law, with a pompous gesture arrested him, and, leading him to the margin of the little lake :

"Monsieur le Duc," said Moulinet, "I see, with vexation, that you are singularly abusing the good understanding that I am trying to maintain with M. Derblay, so as to . . ."

"So as to ?" repeated the Duke, regarding Moulinet from head to foot with remarkable impertinence.

"In the first place," cried the late Judge at the Tribunal de Commerce, quite losing his patience, will you I beg, my son-in-law," and he emphasized this word so particularly disagreeable to Bligny, "cease to take with me a certain mocking tone, that I am no longer disposed to support . . ."

"Monsieur Moulinet revolts, he raises the standard of the Consular Magistracy!" said the Duke laughing . . .

"M. Moulinet finds you altogether incorrigible," continued his father-in-law in a louder voice, "with respect to himself and with respect to our host, to whose wife you are making love in a scandalous manner."

"Madame your daughter has she done me the favour to complain of it?" asked the Duke, affecting an exaggerated politeness still more irritating than his ralliery.

"*Ma foi*, no," said Moulinet; "she even appears to care very little about your fidelity . . . and I can understand it!"

"Well! Then?" mockingly said the Duke.

Moulinet turned half round, and, flashing a glance at his son-in-law:

" And morality, Monsieur ?" said he.

"Oh! The morality of the Rue des Lombards!" replied the Duke making a careless gesture.

Moulinet put on an important air.

" The Rue des Lombards has indeed its value," said he. "You know something of it!"

"Oh! Fie, Monsieur Moulinet," cried the Duke, "do not shake thus your big sous. We know that you are rich." And, again eyeing disdainfully from head to foot the late Judge at the Tribunal de

Commerce: " It is your only merit, do
not abuse it ! "

" My merit, in that case," said Moulinet,
quite losing his calmness, " has this advantage over yours that it increases every
day ! As for the rest, I am very good to
interest myself in you. Pursue your
guilty enterprise ! The only result that
you will obtain will be to pick a quarrel
with the husband, and I warn you in
advance that all my sympathy will be
on his side . . ."

" Quite so ! " said the Duke.

" If he kills you," continued Moulinet
who was exciting himself by talking,
" you will have only what you deserve ! "

" The judgment of God ! "

" We will make for you, my daughter
and myself, obsequies worthy of our
fortune, and we will mourn you at

Monaco and at the sea-side, during the customary period."

" In fact, a gay mourning ! "

" Brought on by the inordinacy of your passions . . ."

" Ah ! Monsieur Moulinet ! Let us terminate this ! " interrupted the Duke haughtily, " I ask no advice, and I accept no lessons. For a few minutes your paternal pedantry amused me, but there is enough of it ! "

" Very well, Monsieur," said Moulinet, dominated by the insolence of the Duke, " do as you like, I wash my hands of it."

And shaking his head with an air of dignity, the father-in-law returned towards the salons.

A great movement was taking place upon the terrace. Suzanne had come running to find her brother who was conversing with the Procureur-Général

and the Préfet, and a little breathless,
very agitated :

"It is a deputation of the workmen,"
said she. "There are ten of them; they
ask permission to approach."

" *Mais comment donc !* " cried the Préfet,
whom the Democrat aroused by those
words : " a deputation of workmen," was
excited. "A little popular demonstra-
tion . . . It is perfect ! "

"He is going to ask them to play the
Marseillaise !" murmured the Trésorier-
Payeur smiling.

Philippe advanced towards the workmen :

"Ah! It is you, Gobert!" said he
recognising his oldest foreman, clad
in his clothes for great days, his hat
in his hand, bearing an enormous
bouquet, and smiling with a troubled
air . . .

"Come forward, my good fellow, and you also, my friends."

Gobert, a tall old man with white hair, remained planted on the same spot, petrified at the sight of all these elegant people standing upon the terrace, and examining him with curiosity."

"Go, then," murmured his comrades, drawn up behind his back. "Go, then! as it is thou who hast to speak."

But he, paralyzed by an unconquerable emotion, gazed, his eyes wide open, immovable, as if he were indeed changed into stone.

It was Suzanne who broke the spell, by going gently to take the hand of the old workman, whom she had known since she was a baby, to lead him to Claire. The foreman bowed before Madame Derblay, and, very troulbed, seeking for words,

although he had learned his little discourse
by heart !

" As the Patron permits it, Madame,"
said he, " deign to accept this bouquet
that I am charged to offer you, in the
name of all my .comrades, wishing you
many happy returns of your *fête* . . .
You must know that at Pont-Avesnes,
there are eighteen hundred of us who owe
all that we have to your husband, who
has built us houses, schools, an infirmary,
who treats us like his children . . . And,
do you see, we are grateful to you for the
happiness that you give him ! "

The words were strangled in the throat
of Gobert, overpowered by his feelings.
Shouts and applause broke out with
vehemence. The Préfet had given the
signal, by turning towards Claire and her
husband, with a smile full of approbation.
Claire had started, on hearing the foreman

speak of the happiness that she gave to Philippe. Thus, from all sides, everywhere and always, this ironical praise reached her.

The tumult was appeased. Gobert freed from his bouquet, still remained planted before M. and Madame Derblay.

"But," continued he, "I have something else to say . . . The country is going to be called on to elect a Deputy . . ."

At these words, Moulinet took a step forward, as if his interests were being attacked. The Préfet drew himself up and darted around him a look of authority.

"And we have come," continued Gobert, "to beg the Patron to let himself be entered for the circumscription of Pont-Avesnes."

Moulinet gave an immense sigh of relief.

" The circumscription adjoining mine,"
cried he, " bravo ! "

A tempest of hurrahs and acclamations,
coming from outside the gate of the principal court, made an echo to the voice of
their old foreman. The workmen of the
Foundry, in their Sunday clothes, with
their wives and their daughters,were pressing forward, assisting from a distance at
the manifestation that they had prepared.

" Open the gate," said Philippe, " let
every one come in."

And, in an instant, a joyous wave swept
into the gardens, overflowing into the
park, under the Venetian lanterns, which
lighted with their many-coloured rays the
dark alleys and the mysterious recesses
ornamented with statues.

" These good people have had an excellent idea," said the Préfet graciously.
" M. Derblay is one of us; he is a liberal,

in the best acceptation of the word. To every one, his name signifies: science, probity, work and liberty!"

"That is a candidateship that I support," added Moulinet. "We two shall monopolize the district. I will work my farmers, committees, meetings, speeches; that is my affair. We shall carry off the election with a high hand!"

"Well! my dear Préfet, it seems to me that we are doing a little official canvassing!" said a martial voice behind the majestic Monicaud. The Préfet turned, as if his foot had been trampled upon, and found himself face to face with the General, who was fixedly regarding him with a bantering air. The representative of the Civil Administration smiled at the representative of the Military Administration.

"Well! my dear General, when one

has dined so well with people, one cannot appear to wage war against them over the dessert! After-dinner politeness!"

Then, pirouetting upon his heels, he muttered between his teeth: "Begone, Pretorian!"

"I accept, my friends," said Philippe, "the honour that you confer upon me. Not in an ambitious end,—you know that I seek but few opportunities of advancing myself,—but because I hope once more to have it in my power to be useful to you."

There was a great tumult; shouts arose from the crowd, and, for two minutes, nothing could be seen but arms frantically waving hats and caps. Then the noise fell little by little. Claire advanced in her turn:

"As to me, my friends," said she, "I thank you from the bottom of my heart for your kind thought. And you, Gobert, as you are the oldest workman at the Foundry, for yourself and all your comrades, come and salute me."

And gracious, smiling, she turned her cheek to the confused old foreman, tortured in his black frock-coat a little tight, his face crimson under his white hair. Gobert approached her, and, with as much precaution - as if the sweet countenance of Claire had been burning, like the red-hot iron that the workmen were accustomed to hammer, he kissed the young woman.

"Oh! Madame," said the poor fellow, not being able to restrain a tear, "the Derblays have always been good people, and you are indeed worthy of being one of the family."

Claire cast at her husband a glance of triumph. The words of Gobert seemed to have re-fastened the bonds which united her to Philippe.

Athénaïs tittered, whispering with La Brède and du Tremblaye :

" Well! This is quite charming: we are swimming in Socialism."

A great shout cut short the speech of the Duchess. Philippe had given orders to roll several barrels of wine into the park, and had sent to seek the band of the country. In an instant, a platform was extemporized with planks. And, raised upon this scaffolding, the musicians sent out into the night the strident tones of their instruments. The vine-dressers from the hill, attracted by the sound, came to mix with the workmen from the Foundry, and the old hostility that had divided the country into two camps was on the way to disappear. In the wide alleys, by the light of the many-coloured lanterns, which shone like fantastic flowers, under the gloomy foliage of the trees, that moving and clamorous multitude resembled a swarm of black ants.

Suddenly the darkness was broken by a brilliant light, and the first bomb of a display of fire-works, ordered and prepared with great mystery by the Baron, burst noisily in the sky, showering upon the astonished crowd a dazzling rain of golden stars. Then the rockets with their trains of fire rushed hissing into the darkness, and the clumps of trees in the park were illuminated by the green and red brightness of Bengal lights.

The musicians ceased playing, and, their instruments upon their knees, from the highest part of the scaffolding, followed with their eyes the capricious flight of the fiery serpents and the wonderful spouting of the Roman candles.

The charming du Tremblaye, who never failed to seize an effect, warbled in a high voice the first words of the popular song:

" Petit Pierre, hausse-moi,
     Que je voie la fusée volante . . . "

The Préfet, turning towards Moulinet, said to him with enthusiasm:

"Do you see how well the red comes out in fire-works! What a beautiful colour!"

"I like quite as well the green," replied the late Judge, who had not caught the allusion.

"It is the colour of hope," said graciously the Trésorier-Payeur, bowing to Moulinet.

The father of the Duchess understood. He was quick-sighted in all that touched his own interests. He regarded the former *viveur* with benevolence, and found him a very agreeable man. Besides, he had the handsomest pair of horses in the Department.

" Well! Monsieur Moulinet," said the Baron who had drawn near, " it is going off well ?. You seem enchanted ! "

" Yes, Baron," replied the late Judge with effusion. " This luxury, these *fêtes*, that animation, all this delights me. I was born for high life. My tastes protest against the injustice of my origin . . . "

" Your mind will suffice to cause it to be forgotten! " said Préfont with imperturbable coolness.

A bright red illumined the sky. They were setting light to the principal design. Under a fiery arch, a little child, delineated by two shades of rose-colour, was crowning a tall woman outlined by two white flames.

" Love crowning industry ! " said the

Baron, who felt compelled to explain the allegory.

"I recognise it!" murmured the majestic Monicaud the ear of the Procureur-Général. "Last year, at Neufchâtel where I was Sous-Préfet, on the evening of the National Fête, they gave us the pink child and the white woman, under this title: 'The future crowning France!'"

"And I," laughingly said the Trésorier-Payeur, "I formerly saw it figure, in a display of fire-works held at Villé-d'Avray, on the *fête* of Dr. Thomson, the celebrated accoucheur, under this appellation: 'Infancy crowning Medicine!'"

A terrible noise and a blinding light broke off the conversation of the guests. The bouquet, a flaming sheaf, mounted into the sky, spreading over the spectators like a dome of fire. A hail of blackened sticks fell upon the heads of the most forward, in the midst of screams and laughter. Then the sky again became dark, and the park, mildly lighted by the Venetian lanterns, regained its usual aspect. As if an invisible hand had given the signal, the instruments of the band brayed out in unison, throwing to the night wind the first bars of a quadrille. A silence succeeded, interrupted by the joking voice of a *gamin* crying : " Take your places for the quadrille ! "

Athénaïs was suddenly seized by the caprice of a *grisette :* she had a wild desire to dance among these peasants. It was so imperious that, her eyes flashing, her face animated, she turned to Philippe, and bending towards him :

" Oh ! Monsieur Derblay, let us open this *bal champêtre !* . . . It will be charming . . . Come, you will dance with me ! "

Philippe remained motionless, hesitating between the wish to refuse and the dread of being discourteous. He exchanged a glance with Claire.

The young woman paled on witnessing this fresh and challenging advance of the Duchess. She thought that the measure was full. And then, she had vowed to herself not to permit Athénaïs to take possession of Philippe. She waited however undecided, anxious, fearing to displease her husband. A mocking voice sounded in her ear, the abhorred voice of the Duke :

" Do you see ? " said he.

And, with a gesture, he pointed out Athénaïs leaning towards Philippe and holding him under the caressing glance of her eyes.

Claire shuddered with grief and with shame. Her suffering was increased

tenfold by the imprudent intervention of
the Duke. At this precise moment, as if
their destiny had at last reached a climax,
the eyes of Philippe met those of Claire.
The young woman, in the glance of her
husband, read so plainly compulsion and
weariness, that she was carried on by an
irresistible impulse. She took three steps,
and, lightly touching the arm of Athénaïs
who was repeating : " We shall open the
ball together, shall we not ?"

" Pardon me, if I oppose thy projects,"
said Claire coldly. " But I wish to speak
for a single instant with thee."

" To speak ?" said the Duchess with
surprise mingled with *ennui.* " How so,
immediately ? "

" Immediately," insisted Claire.

" It is urgent then ? "

" Very urgent."

Athénaïs looked earnestly at her enemy.

Claire sustained this glance with such firmness that the Duchess, troubled, foreseeing some grave event, lowered her eyes, and, in an affectedly mild voice:

"What is it then, *ma chère belle?*" asked she, trying to take the hand of Claire.

"Follow me, and thou wilt know," steadily answered Madame Derblay.

And without adding a word, without turning towards Philippe, Claire, resolute, but with heart beating, drew away Athénaïs into the small deserted salon.

They remained, for a second, standing, like two adversaries ready to come to blows. In the distance, under the foliage, the band on the extemporized orchestra was beginning to play, and the dull murmur of the excited crowd reached the Château in confused bursts. All the guests had descended to the Park.

Athénaïs and Claire, trusting to their own strength, were once again in presence of each other and alone.

"Wilt thou not sit down?" said Madame Derblay in a curt voice.

"It will be long then?" said the Duchess, half suffocating an impertinent yawn.

"I hope not," replied Claire.

Athénaïs threw herself back in an arm-chair. She stretched out her foot, fixed her eyes on the jet ornamented toe of her shoe, and moving it slowly made it glitter under the light of the lustres, appearing to attach no importance to that which Claire had to say to her.

"I have to ask a favour of thee," began Madame Derblay.

"Am I so happy as to be able to oblige thee?" asked Athénaïs carelessly.

"Yes. The other day, at that chase in

the forest, when thou didst take away my husband with thee, thou didst ask me if it displeased me, and if I was not a little jealous . . ."

The Duchess struck a little sharp stroke with her heel upon the inlaid floor and said:

" I was joking ! "

" Well ! Thou wast wrong," declared Madame Derblay, "for thou didst speak the truth."

Athénaïs, extremely astonished, ceased to lie back in her chair and stood upon her guard.

" Thou, jealous ? " said she.

" Yes."

" Of me ? " emphasized the Duchess.

" Of thee ! " repeated Claire. And with a constrained smile, she added : " Thou seest that I am frank. It seems to me that my husband occupies himself

with thee more than is becoming, and I
address myself directly to thee so that
thou canst put a limit to his assiduities,
to which thou evidently attachest no
value, but which to me are very painful."

"Oh! Dear little one," cried Athénaïs,
turning towards Claire with a vivacity full
of the most tender interest: "What!
thou dost suffer and thou sayest nothing!
But dost thou not exaggerate a little? I
can truly remember nothing to cause thy
vexation. M. Derblay is very amiable,
he appears to take pleasure in conversing
with me, but that sympathy between
people of the same family is not surprising,
and there is nothing wrong in it."

"I suffer from it!" said Claire with
persistence.

The little Duchess rose and, in a tone
pointed as a dagger:

"My dear friend, it is of thy husband

that thou must ask the remedy for thy trouble. I can do nothing ! "

" Yes, thou canst break off that intimacy."

Athénaïs fell back languidly into the depths of her chair. She saw now to what Claire wished to come. So, it was a laying down of arms that she required. The young woman softened the sharpness of her voice, and, with an amenity more exasperating than her past stiffness :

" And how shall I be able to arrive at it ? By receiving coldly thy husband ? In the first place, that would impose on me a very ungrateful task. And, then, dost thou really think the means efficacious ? "

She smiled while thus speaking, with the air of bravado of a woman sure of her ascendency.

" Therefore," resumed Claire with her

tranquil serenity, "it is not that which I wish to propose to thee."

"What is it then?"

Madame Derblay hesitated a little, then said boldly:

"It is to absent thyself for some time from our house."

Athénaïs bounded from her seat, and, ceasing to control herself:

"Dost thou mean it?" cried she.

"Yes," said Claire with as much sweetness as her rival had of asperity. "And it is as a prayer that I ask it of thee. Accuse me of being mad; but do that: it will be for my happiness."

"And under what pretext wilt thou that I absent myself?" pursued Athénaïs. "What will be said of a separation so abrupt that it will resemble a quarrel?"

"We will charge ourselves with explaining it in a satisfactory manner."

The persistency of Claire greatly embarrassed Athénaïs. She believed that Madame Derblay was stronger than she had thought her, and that, if she allowed herself to be drawn into making the slightest concession, all would be lost. She resolved to settle it at once and for ever.

"We should not succeed," said she. "And it would be disastrous for me. Thou hast been frank: I will be the same. I am new to the world into which the Duc de Bligny has caused me to enter, I am pleased with it, and it is my intention to keep in it the position that I have already known how to win. But people in that world are very hypercritical. So thou understandest that if the family of my husband showed me coldness, they would find in it an opportunity of discussing me. They are so jealous of my actions! And

adieu to my dreams! If thou hast thy
love, I have my ambition. I can understand that thou art anxious to protect the
one, suffer me to protect the other."

Claire began to tremble. She only
restrained herself with difficulty. The
longing came to her to seize that wretch
and to crush her.

" So, thou refusest ? " said she in a
suffocated voice.

" Against my will. But, candidly, put
thyself in my place ! "

The irony was so cutting that Athénaïs
could not repress a smile.

Claire stepped forward and, ceasing to
subdue her anger :

"I put myself in thy place?" said she
with violence. " It is thou who hast put
thyself in mine, and who wishest again to
put thyself in it ! Since I have known
thee, thou hast pursued me with thy envy

and thy hatred. A girl, thou didst take from me my betrothed ; a woman, thou seekest to take from me my husband ! I did not know how to keep the one, I know how to tear from thee the other ! "

" Ah ! it is thus ! " cried Athénaïs pallid with rage. " Well ! be it so ! Let us raise the mask ! Truly the dissimulation was a burden to me ! Yes, since my childhood, I have returned to thee in hatred all the disdain that thou and thy comrades lavished on me. Thou didst crush me for ten years with thy name, thy fortune, and thy mind ! Well ! see ! To-day I have millions, I am a Duchess, and thou hast to ask of me a favour ! "

" Beware ! " said Claire, " I am not of a race to allow myself to be long insulted with impunity."

" And I," replied the Duchess, " I

bear a name which places me above thy anger ! "

" I sh ll state thy conduct towards me ! "

" To whom ? " asked Athénaïs tittering.

" To the world."

" Which ?   Thine to which I have mounted ? Or mine to which thou hast descended ? "

" To that, whichever it may be, where there are honest people, for whom to respect others is a duty, and to make oneself respected is a right.   Before that world, dost thou hear ?   I shall repeat aloud all that I have said to thee.   I shall show thee as thou art. And we shall see if the name that thou bearest, however great it may be, will suffice to hide thy vileness and thy false-hood."

The Duchess wished to answer.   She

vainly sought for a reply in her heart filled with gall. Her lips only emitted a hissing. Reduced to silence, she attempted at least to insult with a gesture. But she saw, before her, Claire so menacing, her eyes flashing and her hands agitated, that she was afraid. She recoiled and, lowering her voice :

" It is a scandal that thou seekest ! "

" It is an execution that I intend to perform ! One last time, wilt thou consent to that which I ask thee ? "

" No ! A hundred times no ! " repeated Athénaïs, gnashing her teeth.

" Then, thou shalt see ! "

Steps were heard upon the gravel of the terrace, and a sound of joyous voices entered through the windows of the salon. Upon the perron, Philippe appeared, giving his arm to the Baroness. The Duke, laughing with La Brède, followed, preceding Moulinet, who had attached himself to the Baron.

They saw Athénaïs and Claire, pale, shuddering, standing opposite each other. The attitude of the two young women was so significant that all stopped, full of amazement. Then Claire, her head high, feeling that she was in the right, strong through the griefs she had undergone, advanced into the centre of the salon, and pointing to Athénaïs with a withering gesture :

" Duke, take away your wife," said she, " if you do not wish me to expel her from my house, before the eyes of the world ! "

Bligny remained impassive, a cold smile passed over his lips. But Moulinet, not believing his ears, haggard, his arms raised towards Heaven, rushed forward.

" Expel my daughter, the Duchess my

daughter!" repeated he with emphasis, as if, in her, they would touch the whole Aristocracy of France.

Athénaïs, turning to the Duke, cried in a piercing voice:

"Monsieur, do you allow me to be insulted in this way, without defending me?"

Bligny stepped towards Philippe, with perfect calmness.

"Do you approve, Monsieur," said he, " of that which Madame Derblay has just said to the Duchess? Are you disposed to apologize for it, or are you prepared to take the responsibility?"

It was clear, polite, and cutting as steel.

Claire bent upon her husband a look of anguish. Would Philippe condemn her, or would he boldly take her part? She had a moment of horrible uncertainty, during which she suffered more than she had ever suffered before.

At the voice of Bligny, the Ironmaster approached. His tall figure displayed in all its manly vigour. His height surpassed by a head, that of the Duke. Then, gravely and with an energy that made those start who heard him:

" Monsieur le Duc, whatever Madame Derblay may do, whatever reason she may have for doing it, I consider all that she does as well done ! "

The Duke bowed with incomparable elegance; he turned to La Brède, to whom he made a sign, and said :

" It is understood ! "

Then, offering his arm to Athénaïs, who was confounded, he left the room, followed by Moulinet, who was distracted, and by the faithful La Brède, who was murmuring :

" Devil of an affair! two cousins! Bligny is the one insulted; he will choose pistols. The Ironmaster is a dead man!"

Claire, seeing her rival withdraw humiliated and conquered, did not dream of the terrible consequences that would follow her bold stroke. She gave a cry of triumph, and going to her husband, with passionate gratitude:

" Oh! thank you, Philippe!" said she. And vaguely extended her arms to him.

In an instant her fervour died away. She saw her husband again become impassible.

" You owe me no thanks," said he, " In defending you, it was my own honour that I defended."

And Claire remaining dumb and gloomy.

" Do not forget that we have guests here," continued he, " and that no one must suspect that which has just taken place."

He offered his arm to the Baroness, whose nerves were so shaken that she had at the same time the desire to laugh and to weep. Claire brushed away a tear that was falling down her cheek, and, smiling sadly at the Baron, who had waited with her:

"Come," said she, "as it must be so, let us go and dance!"

————

CHAPTER VI.

THE night appeared cruelly long to Claire. Returned to her apartment, she understood the full gravity of the situation, and was dismayed. Truly, she had acted in the plenitude of her right. Braved, menaced, outraged in her home by a pitiless enemy, she had revolted and driven her away. But her private quarrel had become general. Philippe was constrained to undertake her defence, and she now saw him opposed to the Duke. She had before her eyes the enigmatic smile of Bligny when he said: "It is understood." That smile made her shudder. Claire knew what a dangerous adversary was Bligny. If it should come to a duel, would not Philippe incur the risk of a frightful danger? At the end of the evening, she saw, Octave and the Baron conferring with La Brède and Moulinet. She questioned the Baron and her brother; they answered evasively, in an ambiguous manner, stating that the conversation aimed at an arrangement.

Claire wondered what arrangement could be brought about between these two men who hated each other. The Duke had plainly stated the terms of the question: Either an apology or the responsibility, that is to say, satisfaction. The young woman did not entertain for a single minute the idea that her husband would apologize. It was therefore a duel.

Claire was of a courageous race, whose women had never paled at the clashing of arms. One of her ancestors, a Bligny, scoured the hollow roads of La Vendée

with the bands of Stofflet, using his car-
bine, at every opportunity, to shoot down
the *Bleus.* Her father, the Marquis de
Beaulieu, at the age of sixteen, was shut
up in the Pénissière, and at the end of
three days, was found under the ruins of
the farm, his arm broken by a ball. She
inherited their courage. But if she did
not dread death for herself, she dreaded
it for Philippe. Superstition was mingled
with her fears. She fancied that the
union, between the Ironmaster and herself,
was marked with black by destiny. She
had a presentiment that if her husband
fought, he would be killed. And terrible
pictures passed before her eyes.

She saw, upon the turf spotted with
blood, Philippe stretched lifeless, and the
Duke standing,—the pistol still smoking in
his hand,—laughing his wicked laugh.
Wherefore the pistol? Wherefore that

dangerous weapon? She told herself repeatedly that perhaps they would fight with swords. Always, she saw the two men pistol in hand; she heard the double detonation, a light blue smoke mounted into the air, and Philippe, wounded to death, fell heavily upon the grass.

She wished to drive away this nightmare which pursued her waking, and went to the window. The air was sweet, the night beautifully clear, the sky glittering with stars. In the trees of the park the Venetian lanterns, gradually dying out, were reanimated at moments by a puff of wind, and shone in the obscurity like red points. She saw with horror in these red points, spots of blood. Appalled, she closed her window, drawing the curtains so as no longer to perceive that sinister light.

Claire began to walk around her room,

thoughtful, absorbed, turning over in her
mind the lugubrious apprehension of the
death of Philippe. She surprised herself
by speaking aloud, saying : "I bring misfortune to all who approach me!" The
sound of her voice in the silence terrified
her. She stretched herself upon a couch
and tried to read. But a bell ringing in
the distance tolled in her ears, like a
funeral knell.

She wished then to go to Philippe's
room to know what he was doing. She
crossed the small salon on tip-toe, and
went to the door of her husband's apartment. All was silent and dark; no sound,
no light. She believed that he slept, and
that idea reassured her a little. She
returned to her room, and passed the rest
of the night, between sleeping and waking,
in a state of agitation that nothing could
calm.

Philippe was not in his room and he was not asleep. He had shut himself in his study, situated on the ground floor, below the chamber of Claire. He was not ignorant that the encounter between the Duke and himself would be serious. The interviews had taken place the same evening between the four seconds, and the affair, though grave, being of extreme simplicity, the preliminaries had been rapidly settled.

Notwithstanding the tearful supplications of Moulinet, who wished at any price to avoid a duel, a meeting was arranged for eight o'clock in the morning. The spot chosen was the boundary of the woods of Pont-Avesnes and of La Varenne, at an equal distance from the two residences, at that same Rond-Point of the Ponds which, a few days before, was resounding with the joyous exclamations and the laughter of the huntsmen feasting on the sumptuously-prepared luncheon.

The weapon chosen by the Duke was the pistol. The distance thirty paces, to fire till one or the other should be disabled. Philippe accepted these conditions without reluctance. Although he had practised but little with the pistol, he was a first-rate shot with a gun. And sure of his quick sight, he thought with a savage joy, that, if he risked receiving death, he was nearly sure to give it. Between these two men, endowed with equal courage and with well-tried coolness, it was impossible to choose beforehand the victor. But it was quite certain that one of the two was condemned.

Alone, by himself, having perhaps no more than a few hours to live, Philippe yielded to a train of deep meditation. He honestly made the examination of his conduct. One thought troubled him : he feared that he had been too harsh with Claire. At this supreme hour, he felt a deep pity for that troubled soul who had purified herself in her own tears. He saw her now filled by the thought of himself. The haughty woman who had so rudely repulsed him had melted into a humble woman, tender and devoted. The hard trial that he had made her undergo was ended. And he had a right to believe that, living, Claire would devote herself entirely to his love, dead, entirely to his memory.

This was the goal that he had proposed to himself, and feeling that he had attained it, he grew calmer. In the depth of his conscience he did not regret having hammered without truce that character of bronze, so as to mould it to his will. He saw in the result obtained a guarantee for the happiness of Claire, if fortune were favourable to him and if he returned safely. Abandoned to herself, in the disorder of her mind, she had assuredly been unhappy. Too intelligent not to understand that she had spoiled her life, too proud to own that the fault was entirely hers, she had lived devoured by bitter rancours, and had become soured by unavailing regrets. The lesson that he had given was salutary. She was re-gathered, re-found, and re-conquered. And now she was ripe for happiness.

Alas! At the moment when, the work of her regeneration accomplished, Claire might see a smiling future open before her, would adverse fate plunge her into despair?

A sound of steps, over his head in the silence of the night, made Philippe start. He listened. It was a walk regular, uninterrupted, automatic, that of the poor woman who was suffering such cruel anguish, separated from him only by the thickness of a plank, but nevertheless so far off through the implacable will of an outraged husband.

In each vibration of the floor trodden by the foot of Claire, Philippe divined the horrible agitation of the young woman. He fancied he saw her walking around that chamber, her eyes dry, her features contracted, her hands trembling, with that disordered air, that he had seen so often in the madness of her grief or of her anger. He felt his heart swell. For the first time he found himself weak before his love. And his throat tightened, his temples throbbing, he was seized with a violent wish to go to that woman whom he adored and who was not yet his own. Like a child he gave himself reasons to justify

his desire. Should he not be mad to risk
death before having taken her into his
arms, before having buried his lips in the
perfumed tresses of her golden hair?
He had only to speak a word and she
would fall upon his heart. The day was
yet far off. He could taste the despaired-
of delights of a night of love perhaps
without a morrow. At that ardent
thought, he had a vertigo; and trembled.
He took several steps. Already, his hand
touched the door, when a return of his
self-command arrested him.

Was it indeed he who was going to
allow himself to be drawn into such a
mean weakness? After so many sufferings endured, at the last moment, should
he fail in courage? That woman whom
he had subdued, conquered, should he
lower himself so far as to go to beg of
her a few hours of degrading voluptuous-

ness? He was at the epoch which ought, materially and morally, to decide the whole of his life. If he survived, Claire was indeed his own, without evasions for the present, without fears for the future. If he should die, he would remain before her eyes, grand, proud, and implacable. A daring gambler, he would risk the completion of the game. All or nothing. An existence of perfect happiness, or death cold and silent. And resolute, he returned to seat himself at his writing-table.

Over his head, Claire continued her feverish walk. He heard her open the door, cross the salon and, with a stealthy step, go as far as his room. A smile passed over his lips. He listened attentively. At the end of an instant, Claire again crossed the salon and returned to her apartment. Thus, like

himself, she had dreamed of a reconciliation, and, like himself, she had paused. He
understood then how much, by going to
her, he would have fallen from his ele-
vation. He would cease to be the
superior man dominating all by his will,
and would become the vulgar being at
the mercy of his passions.

A feeble light, announcing the day,
recalled him to the worldly cares which
ought to occupy his last moments. He
wished, if he vanished from the earth,
to give to his sister a firm support. He
was able to appreciate the solid qualities
of the Marquis de Beaulieu. In this
young man, he had divined a sensible
mind and a good heart.

If he had responded by a refusal to
the request addressed to him by Claire,
it was only to remain faithful to his
conjugal tactics, and, to strike a blow

harder than all the others upon the heart
of his wife. He felt, at this moment, the
definitive crisis approaching, and he
promised himself to repair speedily the
wrong that he had done to Octave.
Suzanne, moreover, loved him. And at
the thought of causing grief to that child
who had made the sweetness of his life,
his heart melted.

. He resolved to marry the two young
people, and, in order to give more
solemnity to his consent, he lent to it
a testamentary form. Tranquil and self-
collected, he made his dispositions, he
divided his fortune into two parts, one
for Suzanne, the other for Claire, pray-
ing "his dear wife to consent to accept
it, as a *souvenir* of the deep tenderness
that he had vowed to her." He chose,
from amongst his engineers, a manager
upright, and capable to occupy his place.

And, having provided for everything, he thought of sleeping for a few moments. He must have his hand steady and his glance sure. He stretched himself upon the large leather divan and, sighing deeply, closed his eyes.

At the Château of La Varenne the emotion was great, Athénaïs returned from Pont-Avesnes in a state of unutterable rage. At the moment when the woman whom she hated seemed to be definitively overthrown and at her mercy, a vigorous stroke brought her again to her feet, haughty and triumphant. And it was she, the Duchess de Bligny, who was humiliated, expelled, conquered! For she could not conceal from herself that this glaring rupture would do to her irreparable harm.

The whole of the Duke's family would be on the side of Claire. The motives of the Meeting would become known and her disgraceful expulsion would be related, commented on, exaggerated, by a world who detested her. At that thought, Athénaïs ground her teeth, and the desire for carnage overran her heart. She longed to be in the place of the Duke, so that the sanguinary work might be better and more surely done. She dreamed of Claire a widow. She saw her in black, pale, weeping, cursing the hour when she had insulted her rival. She thought that by striking her through the husband whom she loved, she would reach even to the source of her life. Athénaïs burst into a horrible laugh, violently dashed her fan and her gloves upon the table of the salon into which she had just entered, and, turning to Moulinet and the Duke who were silently regarding her :

"That man who defends her who has insulted me," said she with rage, "you must kill him ! "

There was an instant of stupor. Moulinet, overwhelmed by the vindictive exclamation of his daughter. The Duke, astonished to find in Athénaïs an intensity of hatred equal to his own. Nevertheless he reproached the Duchess for having brought about a scene, which had terminated, for her and for himself, in a humiliating retreat. He blamed her for not having known how to restrain herself. Habituated to the perfidies courteously concealed and to the hatreds hidden under smiles of his aristocratic world, he found Athénaïs shockingly vulgar and unskilful. Finally, the attitude *à la Borgia*, taken by the young woman, set his nerves on edge. He regarded her tranquilly, and in a light tone :

" Kill that man! You speak of it at your ease, *ma chère*. These phrases sound very well on the stage. In ordinary life, they are perfectly ridiculous. Break yourself therefore of these big words and of these violent gestures! "

Then, with a cold smile :

" Moreover, you may be certain that I shall do my best in order to give you satisfaction."

" Permit me, Monsieur le Duc," then said Moulinet, emerging from a painful meditation. " I see you disposed to push things to extremities . . . "

" Did you not hear your daughter, *cher monsieur ?* " said Bligny coldly. " Do you think me so little attentive to my duties as not to defend my wife ? "

" There is no question of that," continued Moulinet. " You have, I must recognise it, acted with perfect correctness.

But my daughter is mad to excite you to violence. It is to conciliation that she should exhort you. All may still be arranged. A passing disagreement between two friends, a slight quarrel between two cousins. They will embrace and it will be at an end. But a duel, a scandal, a rupture! You do not weigh the consequences! For you they are enormous! And for me? . . . For me they are disastrous! . . . You are destroying my success as a candidate!"

Notwithstanding the gravity of the situation, the Duke could not prevent himself from laughing. Athénaïs, buried in an arm-chair, coiled up like a viper, emitted a disdainful hissing.

"Pardon, Monsieur le Duc," pursued Moulinet with authority, "I have done enough for you, I think, to be able, in my turn, to make some claims. This deplorable affair must be arranged. Every day the like disputes take place which terminate in a pacification. It is easy. We must draw up a little *procès-verbal*, in which Madame Derblay will declare that she withdraws what she has said. My daughter will withdraw her reply. You, my son-in-law, you will withdraw your provocation, and each withdrawing something, there will only rest . . ."

"That we withdraw ourselves," said the Duke.

"This could be easily done."

"Not when it is a question of persons such as M. Derblay and myself. Believe me, Monsieur Moulinet, impose silence on your excellent heart. Stifle the complaints of the alarmed candidate, and allow things to proceed as they have been settled . . . I must wish you good-night;

I have to speak with La Brède before sleeping."

And saluting with tranquillity his wife and his father-in-law, the Duke left the salon.

Moulinet took several steps towards Athénaïs.

"Let us see, my dear child!" stammered he.

The Duchess, cold and pale, without even glancing at him, rose and, pushing open with an irritated hand the door of her room, she disappeared. Moulinet shook his head with melancholy, and, for the first time, owned to himself that there existed difficulties which could not be surmounted by money.

"The night brings wisdom," said he; "to-morrow it will be day, we shall see more clearly."

And, buoying himself up with a vague

hope, he went to stretch himself in the bed of the Emperor Charles-Quint.

The Ironmaster had calmly slept about two hours, when a slight pressure upon his shoulder aroused him. He opened his eyes, and, seeing the Marquis de Beaulieu standing before him, sprang quickly to his feet. It was broad day-light. The hands of the clock pointed to half past six.

" We have time," murmured Philippe.

Never had he felt himself more free in mind, more vigorous in body. It caused him some pride. In that strong-willed being, all that gave proof of his moral strength yielded to him a secret delight. He went to the window and opened it. An air pure and keen, laden with the perfume of flowers humid from the dew, deliciously enveloped him. He let his eyes wander over the park. A light fog, transparent and blue, floated above the trees like a veil. And the sun, already high in the heavens, sparkled on the calm surface of the sheet of water. Nature had adorned herself, as if to *fête* him.

" A beautiful day ! " cried Philippe gaily, in the same tone as if he were upon the point of starting for the chase.

His glance met that of the Marquis, in whose saddened eyes, he read a dumb reproach. The Ironmaster went to his · brother-in-law, and affectionately clasping his hand :

" Do not be astonished," said he, " at finding me this morning careless and almost joyful. I have a presentiment that all will end well for me."

He became grave.

" However, as we must prepare for misfortune, I have made my dispositions. You will find them in this letter."

He showed upon his bureau an envelope

upon which was written the name of Maître Bachelin.

" My old friend and you will be the executors of my will. I have bequeathed to you, my dear Octave, the dearest thing I possess . . ."

A ray of joy illumined the face of the Marquis. The young man wished to speak ; his voice was strangled in his throat, and, seizing Philippe in his arms, he wept upon his shoulder.

" Now, Octave, a little more fortitude," continued Philippe, " I hope that it will be from my hand that you will receive my sister. But if I should not be there, my friend, when you marry her, love her well, she deserves it. Hers is a tender heart that the least grief would break."

His voice had become infinitely sweet, in speaking of that child, to whom he had been a veritable father. He passed his hand over his forehead, and again calm and smiling:

"It is necessary that I dress," said he. "Will you come to my room with me? You will bear me company. And then we will go to find the Baron. I should wish to leave without attracting attention . . ."

Octave lowered his head without answering; then, at the end of an instant, making an effort:

"Philippé, before seeing you, this morning," said he, "I saw my sister . . . Promise me that you will not start without going to her room!"

Philippe. darted at the Marquis an interrogative glance.

"It is inadmissible," continued Octave, "that you should leave without giving her the opportunity of justifying herself in your eyes, if that is possible . . ."

And as the Ironmaster made an abrupt movement of surprise.

" For three days I have known all that has passed between Claire and yourself," gravely said the Marquis. " She has confessed everything to me. I know how culpable my sister has been, Philippe, and I commiserate you, believe me, for having endured such severe chagrin, as much as I admire you for having known how to conceal it. But, I pray you, be indulgent, be kind. It would be worthy of you not to overwhelm that poor despairing woman. You are an energetic man and courageous : one dares to say all to you. Think then that she may see you no more. Do not leave her crushed beneath the double remorse of having destroyed your life, and, perhaps of having sent you to your death . . ."

The Ironmaster became pale and turned

away his face. He took several steps, then, returning to Octave :

" I will do what you ask me," said he. " But that interview will be horribly painful to your sister and to myself. Act in such a way as to shorten it, and facilitate for me the departure, by coming to seek me in her room . . ."

The Marquis made a sign of assent. And clasping tenderly the hand of Philippe, he went out with him.

CHAPTER VII.

IN the early morning the Baroness went to join her friend. She found her, after the terrible agitation of the night, in a state of unconquerable torpor. Madame de Préfont spoke to Claire, without being able to obtain an answer. Her eyes fixed, her mouth contracted, her body inert and motionless, the young woman was crouching upon the sofa. Her whole soul was concentrated in the look, gloomy and distracted, which seemed to be riveted on some frightful vision.

A long while passed thus. The striking of the clock, announcing the march of the hours, each time made Claire start. Except for this movement, except for the

savage brightness of her eyes, one would
have believed her to be sleeping.

The arrival of Octave drew her from
her torpor. She clung passionately to
the hope of seeing Philippe before his
departure. Feverish, her cheeks marked
with two red spots, in a voice monotonous
and as if worn out, she charged the Marquis
to obtain from her husband that supreme
favour.

And from that time she waited, in a
state of renewed agitation, walking incessantly from the window, of which she
raised the curtain to make sure that they
had not deceived her, and that Philippe
was not starting, to the door, at which
she listened hoping to hear him coming.
Anxious, unnerved, and giving to the
terrified Baroness the spectacle of her
increasing frenzy.

Suddenly a sound of steps made her

recoil as if she dreaded to find herself face to face with him whom she was invoking with her whole soul. She paled, a black circle surrounded her eyes, with a gesture she signed to the Baroness to leave her. And stood waiting, trembling, speechless. Philippe entered.

They remained dumb in the presence of each other. He, examining with grief the traces that so much frightful anguish had left upon the face of his wife. She, who, a moment before, had so many things to say to him, seeking to collect her ideas and, in her aching brain, finding nothing but a void.

Claire could bear no longer this oppressive silence, she went towards Philippe, seized his hand between her own and, moaning despairingly, she covered it with tears and kisses.

The Ironmaster had expected an explanation; he was prepared to hear entreaties and prayers. This outburst of grief, that he knew to be sincere, overpowered him. He tried to withdraw his hand upon which he felt the scalding tears of her whom he loved. He could not succeed. He shivered, feeling himself powerless against so much weakness . . .

"Claire," said he in a low voice, "for pity's sake! . . . You trouble me deeply . . . I require all my coolness . . . I pray you to calm yourself . . . Be stronger, spare me, if you care for my life . . ."

At these words, Claire raised her head. The expression of her face was no more the same.

She appeared to have taken a sudden resolution.

"Your life!" said she. "Ah! Rather would I give my own a hundred times.

Wretch that I am! It is I who, through my ungovernable anger, have thrown you into danger. Ought not I to have borne everything? By my sufferings, I expiated my wrongs towards you . . . And in one minute of rage I forgot all. But this duel is senseless . . . It shall not take place, I know how to prevent it . . ."

"And how?" asked Philippe, already beginning to frown.

"By sacrificing my pride to your safety," answered Claire. "Oh! Nothing will dishearten me, as it concerns you . . . I will humiliate myself before the Duchess, if necessary, I will go to find the Duke . . . There is still time."

The features of the Ironmaster contracted.

"I forbid you to do it!" said he with firmness. "You bear my name do not forget it! Every humiliation undergone by you strikes myself. And then, in fine, you must understand that I hate him, that man who has been the cause of my unhappiness! . . . For a year I have dreamed of finding myself face to face with him . . . Ah! Believe me, this day is welcome!"

Claire lowered her head. For a long time she had been accustomed to obey when Philippe commanded. Calmed by that energetic outbreak, he continued with gentleness:

" I appreciate your intentions and I am grateful to you! There was, between us, at the beginning of our married life, a misunderstanding which has cost us both much suffering. I do not think you only responsible for it. It was partly my fault . . . I did not know how to understand you . . . I did not know how to sacrifice myself . . . I loved you too much! . . . But I do not wish to leave you with the ` thought that I have cherished anger against you . . . You may be at peace Claire. In your turn pardon me the pain that I have caused you, and bid me adieu . . : "

At these words, the face of Claire beamed with delight. And, raising her hands to Heaven in a transport of passionate gratitude :

" Forgive you, I ! " cried she. " But do you not see that I adore you ? Have you not divined it, for a long time, in the agitation of my voice, in the confusion of my eyes ? "

She had drawn near Philippe, and throwing her beautiful arms round his neck, rested her golden head upon his shoulder, intoxicating him with the perfume of her hair, and with the ardour of her glance.

She spoke now as in a dream.

"Ah! Do not go! If thou didst know how I love thee! Stay here, with me, all my own! We are so young, we have so much time to be happy! Of what importance to thee are that man and that woman who hate us? We will forget them. Let us go, wilt thou,· far from them? There it will be happiness, life, and love."

Philippe gently unfastened her clinging arms, and, withdrawing from her :

"Here," said he simply, "is duty and honour."

Claire moaned. The hideous reality had again taken possession of her. She saw, in an instant, the Duke, his pistol in his hand and laughing, with a wicked expression. She wished to spring forward, to make a last effort, to retain Philippe in spite of himself. She cried :

"No! . . . No! . . ."

At the same moment, the door opened and Octave appeared. He made a sign to Philippe and withdrew. Claire understood that the time for departure had come. It was as if a veil which darkened her mind had been suddenly torn away. She knew that all was over. And sinking upon the breast of her husband, she clung to him with convulsive strength.

"Adieu," murmured the Ironmaster.

"Oh! Do not leave me thus! Not with that icy word! . . . Tell me that you love me! Do not go without having told it to me! . . ."

Philippe remained unshaken. He had owned that he pardoned her; he would not say that he loved her. He put Claire from him, walked towards the door, and, upon the point of going out:

"Pray to God that I may return

living !" said he, throwing to her in these words a supreme hope.

That was all. The young woman uttered a cry that quickly brought the Baroness. The carriage which conveyed away the Ironmaster was rolling heavily down the avenue.

Claire, without troubling herself at the presence of the Baroness, fell back upon her couch, her head buried in the cushions, wishing neither to see nor to hear, dreaming of suspending her life during the terrible hour that was about to pass. She remained thus for several minutes.

A sweet voice made her rise abruptly. Suzanne, tapping at the door, said :

"May one come in ?"

Claire exchanged a sorrowful glance with the Baroness. They must dissimulate, must force themselves to deceive that child, ignorant of the truth. Through the half-open door, the fresh and merry face of Suzanne appeared.

" Come in, my child," said Claire.

And, by a prodigious effort of will, she became smiling.

" What! you are not dressed?" cried the young girl, seeing her sister-in-law still in a *peignoir*. " I have already made the tour of the park in the little carriage."

Suzanne ran about the chamber, foraging everywhere with the playfulness of a kitten.

" Stay!" said she, " I have just met Philippe with the Baron and M. Octave. They were in a closed carriage . . . They had a strange manner . . . Where can they be going in that way, all the three?"

Claire reddened and paled alternately. The cold dew of anguish stood on her forehead. Each word of Suzanne tortured her.

"Oh! If my husband was there," said the Baroness, "it is that there is an experiment in question . . . A visit to the quarries . . ."

"In what direction were they going?" asked Claire in a trembling voice.

"In the direction of the Ponds," answered the young girl. "Perhaps they are going to La Varenne?"

"Oh! no," said the Baroness, "the Duc de Bligny is not likely to leave his room before ten o'clock . . ."

Claire heard no more. In the direction of the Ponds, Suzanne had said. Immediately, the glade, with its carpet of turf, its fences painted white, and, in the distance, the waters sleeping under the hanging branches of the trees, passed before her eyes. This spot lonely and mournful was favourable for a duel. It had a desolate aspect which foreshadowed some tragic scene. It was there that the Duke and Philippe were to fight. She was sure of it, she saw them.

She was again a prey to dreadful agitation, brought on by the wish to be certain. She could not remain still; she seized a gown and put it on hastily. A project, put into execution as soon as conceived, came to her, to which she bent all the power of her will.

" Thou hast finished with the little carriage ? " said she to Suzanne. " Where hast thou left it ? "

" In the stable yard," replied the young girl. " They are unharnessing at this moment."

" I am going to use it. I have to take a drive this morning in the country," quickly continued Claire.

And, without waiting for anything, a

scarf of lace thrown over her bare head, she ran out.

Alone, driving boldly, she started at a rapid pace. The motion, far from calming her fever increased it. She had a frenzied desire for speed, putting her horse to a gallop, she was shaken terribly in the ruts of the forest road, and in danger of breaking everything.

She stopped at nothing, augmenting the rapidity of her pace, her nerves strung, biting her lips, envying the birds their wings, and listening, her respiration impeded by the throbbing of her heart, dreading to hear a sinister report break the stillness of the woods.

The forest was silent. In the distance, the bells of the carriages, passing on the high-road, rang joyously. The mossy carpet of the alley stretching out beneath the feet of the horse, deadened the sound of his steps. A thick steam rose from his flanks, surrounding him like a cloud. Urged beyond his strength, he stumbled and fell. Claire sprang to the ground unhurt, and took her way through the woods. Her instinct warned her that she was approaching her goal: she listened and heard voices.

She cast a rapid glance around her. At twenty yards from her, on the margin of the Ponds, stood the Chinese Kiosque of Monsieur Moulinet, its *plaques* of porcelain mirrored in the water. From thence, Claire could see without being seen. Light as a tracked hind, she glided through the branches, and, mounting the steps which led to the circular gallery, she waited, anxious, dismayed.

In the centre of the Rond-Point, the Baron, taking long steps, was counting the paces in order to mark the distance.

La Brède, aided by Moulinet, pale and distracted, was loading the weapons. Philippe, at the other end of the clearing, walking slowly, was conversing with Octave and the Doctor. The Duke, at three steps from the Kiosque, was chewing a cigar, and cutting off mechanically, with a small cane that he carried in his hand, the tall stalks of the fox-gloves.

With a horrible contraction of the heart, Claire remembered the Rond-Point covered with horsemen, with groups of elegantly dressed women, and the luncheon served by the stately footmen of La Varenne. All, on that day, was gay, brilliant, happy. She was jealous then, but was her jealousy to be compared to the torture that she was enduring at this moment? She had, under her eyes, those two men who through her fault were seeking to kill each other.

In a few seconds one of the two would be stretched upon the grass.

A cloud passed before her eyes. She was obliged to hold by the balustrade to preserve herself from falling. Her faintness was of short duration. She looked again, breathless, with an appalled curiosity.

The two adversaries were now placed. M. Moulinet had just cried in a supplicating voice:

"Gentlemen, for mercy's sake, gentlemen . . . !"

He was led away by La Brède, who severely lectured him in a corner. Octave gave a pistol to Philippe, and quickly drew back. La Brède asked in a firm voice:

"Gentlemen, are you ready?"

The Duke and Philippe answered at the same moment: "Yes."

The young man continued, counting slowly :

" One,—two,—three,—fire ! "

Claire saw the two pistols lowered menacingly. In that supreme second, she lost her reason. An unconquerable impulse urged her forward. With a cry, she cleared at a bound the steps of the Kiosque, and, hurling herself to meet the blow which threatened Philippe, she stopped with her white hand the barrel of the pistol of de Bligny.

There was a ringing report. Claire became pale as death. And shaking madly her wounded and bleeding hand, she sprinkled with large red spots the face of the Duke. Then, sighing deeply, she fell to the ground in a swoon.

There was a moment of indescribable confusion. The Duke recoiled, filled with horror, on feeling fall upon him that warm and crimson rain. Philippe, with a bound, seized Claire, and raising her as if she had been a child, bore her to the carriage which was waiting at the turning of the road.

The eyes of the young woman were closed. Anxiously, the Ironmaster, assisted by the Doctor, tenderly raised the poor mutilated hand. He kissed with adoration that flesh which was suffering for him.

Much affected, the Doctor, with the soft touch of a woman, examined the arm of Claire.

"Nothing broken," said he at last with relief. "We have got off better than we could have hoped. The hand, it is true, will be scarred . . . But Madame Derblay can conceal it by wearing gloves."

He began to laugh, regaining the coolness of an operator. Then, he arranged the cushions of the carriage, so that the young woman might be at ease.

Philippe, still confounded and horror-struck, did not take his eyes from Claire . . . Her prolonged unconsciousness disquieted him. The Baron, speaking to him, brought him back to the situation. La Brède, very agitated, accompanied M. de Préfont.

"I am charged, Monsieur, by the Duc de Bligny, to express to you his deep regret at the misfortune of which he is the involuntary cause. The accident that has happened to Madame Derblay afflicts him seriously, and his ideas have become much modified. It now appears impossible to him to proceed with the affair engaged in. The courage of my friend is above dispute. Yours equally so, Monsieur. We are all men of honour . . . The secret of that which has just passed will be faithfully kept."

The Ironmaster glanced towards the Duke. Bligny, trembling and livid, his back leaning against the fence, was mechanically wiping his face. And each time, with a grievous pang at the heart, he brought away the delicate handkerchief marked with a red stain. He shuddered when he thought that his ball might have struck Claire mortally, have fractured her beautiful forehead, or have wounded her white bosom. At this time, he judged himself severely, he had a horror of all that he had done, and resolved to remove himself for ever from the path of her who, through his fault, had so keenly suffered.

La Brède continued to speak to Philippe with an emotion that was not habitual to him. The Ironmaster understood vaguely that the young man was expressing his personal regret. He allowed him to shake his hand with vigour. And seeing the Duke leave the ground, drawn away by Moulinet, he shoved the Doctor into the carriage, mounted to the box, took the reins, and drove off rapidly.

In the large apartment hung with old tapestry upon which the young goddesses were filling the goblets of the warriors, as during the long illness of Claire, Philippe, silent, was seated at the foot of her bed.

The young woman, a prey to fever, for a full hour not having entirely regained consciousness, was moving upon her pillow. She opened her eyes. Her uncertain glance sought Philippe. The Ironmaster rose quickly and bent down to her. A smile passed over the lips of Claire. With her bare arm she encircled the neck of her husband and drew him tenderly towards her. In her troubled brain the exact notion of things had not yet returned. It seemed to her that her spirit was floating in Celestial space. She did not suffer. A delicious languor had taken possession of her. So low, that Philippe hardly heard it, she murmured:

"I am dead, is it not so, my well-beloved, dead for thee? How happy I am! Thou smilest, thou lovest me! I am in thine arms. How sweet is death! And what an adorable eternity!"

Suddenly the sound of her voice aroused her. An acute pain darted through her hand. She remembered all: her despair, her anguish and her sacrifice.

"No! I am living!" exclaimed she.

She repulsed Philippe, and, regarding him distractedly, as if her life or her death would be decided by a word:

"One word only," said she, "answer! Dost thou love me?"

Philippe showed to her his face radiant with ineffable delight :

"Yes, I love thee," replied he. "There are in thee two women. She who caused me so much suffering is no more. Thou art she whom I have never ceased to adore."

Claire gave a rapturous exclamation, her eyes filled with tears, she clung desperately to Philippe, their lips met, and, in an inexpressible ecstasy, they exchanged their first kiss of love.

THE END.

WYMAN AND SONS, PRINTERS,
GREAT QUEEN STREET, LINCOLN'S-INN FIELDS,
LONDON, W.C.